RIVETINGLY GREAT STORIES VOLUME 4

CONNOR WHITELEY

DEDICATION

Thank you to all my readers without you I couldn't do what I love.

INTRODUCTION

If there is one subgenre of science fiction that I love beyond all others (maybe even space opera but I guess there is a large overlap here) it just has to be far future science fiction. I would almost go as far as saying, it is the only form of science fiction I am really interested in.

I love the idea of humanity managing to come together, not kill or wipe themselves out and grow and develop into a space-faring race that can travel to distance planets and solar systems.

This type of science fiction is almost as old as time in the genre. It has been redone plenty of times with thousands, if not millions, of science fiction authors creating their own Empires and Alliances and other various takes on democratic and tyrannical forces. And I think readers are certainly comfortable with that framework because it is almost a genre expectation, but everyone loves an author who puts their own twist on things to make it their own.

I think that is the reason why I love Warhammer 40,000 because there are so few authors and galactic empires that are so rich and merge aliens, demons and other fantasy and science fiction elements so perfectly.

It is the reason why I like Dean Wesley Smith's Seeders series so much, because it is unique in how he deals with the vastness of space so his characters can fly past galaxies like fence post. I highly recommend after reading this volume and some of my other books that you check out his incredible fiction.

Then finally, I enjoy Kristine Kathyn Rusch's far future series about wreck diving in space and how the characters from the present are busy trying to find an ancient lost culture amongst other things.

Overall, as you can see, the best science fiction that readers love come from an author taking the most basic idea of the genre, like a galactic empire, and putting their own twist on it however the author sees fit.

Therefore, in this volume, you'll read and enjoy twenty different science fiction short stories by me set in the far future. You'll get to see how humanity overcome sustainability issues in three extremely different stories in the form of *A Conversion Problem, A Crash Course Problem* and *Monster Man Didn't Create.*

In addition, you get to explore the depths of space and what happens when something goes wrong in the stories *Powdery Mildew Invasion, Genetics Of A Superhuman* and *The Wooden Man In Dilation.*

All before we explore various theatres of war spread throughout the galaxy, and sometimes war isn't as clear-cut or violent as you would first believe.

And there are plenty of other great, enthralling stories to enjoy.

So please grab your favourite drink and sit back and relax as you're transported to various vivid, imaginative far futures you'll love escaping into, but I'll leave the decision of whether or not you want to live in these harsh, dangerous universes up to you.

TREATY OF DEFEAT

Lawyer Elaine Cars's life would be changed forever today.

Elaine sat inside her little sterile white plastic cubicle on the very top floor of her major law firm on Earth. She loved how the cubicle was always so bright, wonderful and clean unlike so many other places on Earth.

A large black holographic computer and grey hovering desk was in front of her, and Elaine really liked how the black office chair she was sitting at supported her so much better than her old one on the lower levels. She had only gotten the job promotion yesterday so this was her first full day and she seriously loved the new job so far.

It was just brilliant.

She was surprised how her new office chair seemed to cradle her body like the amazing hugs her mother used to give her before the foul cancer took her away.

And the chair supported her back, arms and neck perfectly so that Elaine was really hoping to get rid of the constant aching of her muscles from the poorly designed chairs of the awful lower levels.

Elaine was a little unsure about the sterile whiteness of the cubicle because it was a little unnerving. There was no art, paintings or pictures at all on the walls and her new boss had said that she should only be focusing on her legal work and not silly artwork.

But Elaine had always loved art ever since she was a little kid. To her, art was a way of preserving the human culture, learning about others and seeing the world in a new light.

Elaine shook away the thought and simply focused on her black holographic computer that she was seriously impressed by.

Her old one on the lower levels was so old, full and glitchy that her boss had threatened to sack her three times in the past week because apparently her productivity wasn't high enough. It was only not high enough because of the damn glitchy computer.

Thankfully that shouldn't be a problem up here on this floor, and Elaine loved how as her fingers gently touched the black holographic keyboard, the holograms no longer zapped her like her old ones did.

Every single damn night Elaine used to have to put her fingertips in a tub of ice to stop the pain, the zapping was that painful, but hopefully that wouldn't be a problem now.

Elaine clicked on her computer and was surprised that her caseload was so small today.

When she was working on the lower floors, she used to work forty cases a day and mostly she failed a ton of clients like every single other lawyer on Earth but she liked to believe she tried her hardest on all her cases. It was only yesterday she had helped keep a family together so they weren't ripped apart, she had also helped a family get their innocent daughter off a murder charge and she had convicted a kidnapper.

She helped so many amazing people and that was why she loved her job so much but she wanted to help even more people.

"Welcome Elaine to the Top Criminal Division of Baring & Law," her computer said.

Elaine felt so excited to finally be able to access the top-secret and highly sensitive and dangerous cases that these legendary lawyers dealt with.

But when she went to click on her inbox she watched all her other cases disappear and she was only left with a single case.

She clicked on it.

It was really odd that it took a while for the case file to open and Elaine detected a subtle change in the air. The environmental systems on Earth were meant to be the best in the Imperium but now all she could smell was sugar, caramel and candyfloss. It was a wonderful smell if not a little strange, yet she did love the taste of salted caramel that formed on her tongue.

"Access granted," the computer said.

Elaine had no idea why she needed access to look at her own workload but she didn't care and she simply looked at the file.

She instantly frowned as she read the file. She was going to have to deal with a female Keres, a foul alien abomination that had committed an awful crime against humanity and the Imperium.

Elaine hated the Keres with a passion, they were always so rude, foul and just beasts when compared to humanity. And they were just freaks as well with their magic and Elaine shivered in fear.

It was a very well-known rule in the Imperium that humans should never ever mix with such awful creatures that were sadly allowed to roam around in the Imperium because of the Treaty of Defeat.

The only piece of comfort that Elaine and all of humanity got from the Treaty was that the Keres were certainly second-class citizens and they were to be discriminated against at every single chance that presented itself.

Elaine actually wasn't so sure that was fair or just or right but she was a lawyer now and it was her task to make sure this Keres scum plead guilty to charges of theft.

It was so damn annoying that this scum felt like she had the right to steal from superior humans. That was disgraceful and Elaine was so looking forward to punishing this alien beast.

But she couldn't help but feel like there was more to this story and as much as she wanted to believe everything the Imperium said about the Keres.

She had actually never met one before and she couldn't help but believe there was a tiny chance they weren't everything the posters said they were.

But right now all Elaine was interested in was protecting

humanity from the aliens.

***

Because the Keres were such foul, dangerous and awful creatures, Elaine was really glad they were kept in high-security areas of the law firm so she had to go through more security checkpoints than she cared to think about.

Elaine went down a very long black metal corridor with prison bars lining the corridor and the disgusting Keres prisoners were standing there looking so scared at her, with bright blue prison collars around their awful necks.

Elaine absolutely hated the Keres' appearance. They were humanoid in shape but their chests and waists were a lot thinner and their facial features were more angled and she might have even classed the very fit men handsome if they weren't alien scum.

All the Keres wore black prisoner uniforms that fit their very slim and spinney bodies very well.

Just like everyone else in the Imperium Elaine had lived through the War between humans and Keres, and just like the news reports said Elaine had to agree that the Keres were monsters.

The aliens burnt entire planets in the name of their Empire, they murdered every human they came over and they used their magic for such dark purposes that Elaine often turned off the news at night. All whilst humanity was being angelic, calm and wonderful.

They never killed a Keres that didn't deserve it.

Elaine kept walking down the long corridor until she reached the end of it where a steel door was that opened for her only. She went inside.

The interrogation room was perfect for the female Keres scum that sat on a cold metal chair and rested on her long thin arms on the metal table. Thankfully she was chained and Elaine was not going to order the guards to release her.

The Keres were way too dangerous for that. And Elaine just had to focus on how badly she wanted to protect her friends, family and species from these foul aliens.

As Elaine sat down on the icy cold chair and tucked it in, she had to admit she was surprised that the Keres female looked so scared, human and innocent.

Yet that was something else that the glorious Rex pointed out about the awful Keres, they were masters of fear and manipulation. Elaine couldn't dare allow herself to be manipulated by the alien.

She had to remain strong to protect her species. And all she needed to do was get a confession and then go.

"You are accused of theft," Elaine said.

The Keres looked at her. "Please. I didn't steal anything. The human gave it to me,"

Elaine laughed. "That's what they all say and we all know you Keres are thieves,"

The female Keres shook her head as Elaine got out her holo-slate and looked at the case notes she had made in the lift.

"You were found with two hundred Guards worth of technological gadgets that you stole from a merchant," Elaine said.

"No," the Keres said. "I bought that equipment fair and square. I showed the Justice the receipt and he logged it into evidence,"

Elaine nodded because she wasn't lying and there was a receipt.

"I know but the Treaty of Defeat made it clear. The law states that if a Keres buys something then it doesn't belong to Keres. And if the human wants it back then the Keres must give it back without refund,"

The Keres's foul lips thinned. "I know that but…"

Elaine just couldn't understand how this alien could understand the law and so willingly break it. That was why no one liked the Keres.

It wasn't exactly a confession and Elaine sadly knew it wouldn't make her bosses happy with her.

"It just isn't fair," she said.

Elaine stopped for a moment. She had been given this case to get a guilty verdict and she needed this piece of scum to confess, but she highly doubted she would get it if she didn't fake trust and liking this piece of criminal trash.

Elaine forced herself to smile and looked at the alien. All she needed to do was get the alien to trust her and confess to her crime completely.

"Why did you buy it then?" Elaine asked, trying to sound how she did with humans.

The Keres looked at her like Elaine was a good friend. Elaine really couldn't believe how this species had gotten so powerful if they broke laws and trusted so easily.

"It's my husband's birthday today so I was going to get him a special treat. He fought for the humans in the War and he had always loved those old holo-movies so I was hoping to record one for myself and show him. I have a degree in Keres Film Studies,"

Elaine forced herself not to shiver. The Glorious Rex had shown the Imperium what the Keres called "movies" and it was horrific. There was so much blood, murder and other things that she didn't even want to think about.

And apparently what humans called horror films were comedies to the Keres. That was how messed up the aliens were.

Elaine forced herself to nod and smile. "That's really nice of you. I wished my husband did that for me,"

She didn't have a husband but she had learnt over the years if you wanted to make someone trust you, tell them you were in a relationship. It worked every time.

"Thank you. So I saved for months and months and I travelled here on a cargo shuttle to get the equipment,"

Elaine frowned. "You came on a method of transport that wasn't a dedicated Keres flight?"

The female Keres frowned slightly. "Um, it wasn't that serious. I only wanted to cross into Imperial Space for a day and the Keres flights are two hundred times the price of a cargo shuttle,"

Elaine shook her head. "I'm sorry but the Treaty is clear. Keres can only come into Imperial Space if they board a dedicated Keres flight. It is illegal for you to come on any other transport method,"

The Keres frowned. "And yet you humans can use any method to come into our Empire. You can teleport, use cargo shuttles, tourist shuttles and military transports. How is that fair?"

Elaine shrugged because this wasn't her problem. She only wanted to protect her friends, family and species from the Keres.

The law helped her do that.

The Keres tried to reach across the table but she couldn't and Elaine was so glad about that.

"Please. This isn't right. I pay for those goods, I might not have returned them when asked but that was because this isn't right. The Keres are victimised at every single turn,"

As much as Elaine wanted to leave because she had her confession, she actually wanted to listen for just a moment longer. Because emotionally she couldn't understand where the hell this whacko alien was coming from, but at an intelligence and rational level, the alien made a good point.

"Your species signed the Treaty of Defeat. They could have chosen not to. If you're mad at the laws you are subject to then be mad at your Creator or whatever weird name you have for him,"

The Keres shook her head. "You lie and you don't know your own history. The Keres were forced to sign those documents or your humanity was going to nuke our entire Empire and ten planets of your own,"

Elaine laughed. This alien needed to be locked away desperately. She was a psycho.

"Our Creator could live with the sacrifice and defeat of our species but we wouldn't allow your Rex to annihilate hundreds of billions of his own people and he knew that,"

Elaine just laughed because this alien was just making up so many excuses for her criminal actions, but she couldn't help but feel like she wasn't lying.

Her father had served in the War and even though he had come back a changed man because of the things he had seen, he had been drunk one night and he had mentioned about killing humans.

Elaine had always dismissed the memory but what if her father wasn't wrong?

She just looked at the foul alien scum and shook her head. This wasn't right and this was just another manipulation that the Keres was using on her.

She had her confession and thankfully this alien was going to be locked away for a very, very long time.

Elaine got up to leave but the Keres spoke to her. "I feel sorry for humanity because your Rex pumps out so much hate, propaganda and lies that even you cannot tell the difference between right and wrong. Oh, wow humanity has lost its way,"

Elaine just left the scum in the room because she didn't have time for any more lies.

But deep, deep down Elaine had to admit that the Keres might not be wrong after all.

***

After a great, wonderful and sensational day of working another ten more cases involving the disgusting Keres, Elaine sat back on her delightful chair and sterile white cubicle that stopped her from seeing the other workers that had their own white cubicles and Elaine had to admit today had been weird.

Her bosses had said how great, ruthless and cunning she was because she had managed to get a confession from each of the Keres criminals, but the words of the first Keres had only grown in her mind with each case.

She had interrogated and charged all ten of the other Keres today and if she really had to admit it, they were all for silly petty crimes that humans couldn't actually get charged for.

Like her last case was charging a Keres for "assaulting" a human when all that had actually happened was the Keres had been tripped over by an elderly woman and the male Keres had fallen on top of a female teenager.

The Keres had been arrested and Elaine had charged him for a hundred years to be served on a mining world by making him do forced labour.

And as the wonderful smells of mint, lavender and caramel formed in the air, Elaine couldn't help but wonder if this was right in the slightest. And each of the Keres had told her differing stories to how the Keres Empire had come to sign onto the Treaty of Defeat and none of them matched the Rex's version.

Was it possible that Elaine was lied to?

Elaine had no idea and if she was thinking about this from a legal and historical viewpoint (because she had studied history briefly before the Rex outlawed history) she had to admit it was very, very possible.

But that was a problem for another day, Elaine was one woman in one law firm on one planet of the Imperium. She couldn't do anything about it and if she didn't convict Keres people then she couldn't get paid.

Yet she couldn't deny that it wasn't fair so maybe, just maybe one day she could help change all of that but it was a very, very long way away and Elaine had a large amount of criminals to deal with first.

So Elaine had to return to the job and caseload she loved with a new sense of injustice that she knew would morph into action at some point and the Keres would be saved.

AUTHOR OF AGENTS OF THE EMPEROR SERIES
CONNOR WHITELEY
ENEMY OF HISTORY
A SCIENCE FICTION FAR FUTURE SHORT STORY

ENEMY OF HISTORY

Librarian Aria Pinncock had always loved her library with its immense wooden shelves and dark varnish that stretched on for hundreds of miles and the tourists flocked to see the library just for the shelves alone. You couldn't see wooden shelves anywhere else in the Imperium, and Aria really did love the soft blue carpet. It was just such a strange texture that also wasn't found anywhere else in the Imperium.

She stood on the very bottom of the great wooden staircase that went elegantly up towards the second, third and fourth floors of the immense library that she had come to love so much. The staircase was a real beaut with its solid oak railing that were handcrafted on Earth itself with all sorts of designs that the Rex personally approved for the library.

Aria wasn't really sure that she liked it when the tourists said that the staircase was holy or something because the Rex had apparently touched it himself. But considering just how much propaganda there was in the Imperium, it was impossible to tell.

Aria still loved her job.

The staircase even had a couple of marks, scratches and worn patches where so many great scholars had been working away and going up and down to investigate their latest project.

Aria really had enjoyed her career in academia and she had always liked this library even more. Especially with its rows upon rows of real blue leather-bound hardbacks, as the Head Librarian

Aria was always searching for more but most of the books she bought were confiscated by the Rex.

Damn him.

It was always such a rarity to see real print books these days with their soft leather covers, musty smell and cold to the touch that Aria never wanted to leave her library. It was a place of knowledge and she had seen the first-hand impacts of the Rex's great campaign to suppress knowledge.

People talking, muttering and even shouting caught Aria's attention as a large group of white robbed scholars were walking towards the staircase. Aria didn't allow them to worry her for now.

Aria had gone on holiday plenty of times to the other systems without a librarian like herself that prized knowledge beyond all else. So many millions of people died because their medical care was shambolic, all because the Rex had suppressed important medical textbooks because of the so-called evil knowledge inside certain passages.

Apparently the Rex was going to rewrite all the books he confiscated but Aria had never seen such books.

It was why she had been kicked out of academia and she had lost her history job, her fellow professors and best friends were imprisoned for not agreeing to rewrite history books for Rex and she actually had no idea what happened to them. Aria was only saved because a few decades ago her family were rich, powerful and the Rex liked them a great deal.

Aria hadn't spoken to them for decades, she just wanted to keep them safe. When she started learning about history she never ever imagined it would become a crime.

"Excuse me," a man said.

Aria looked at the man and forced herself not to frown at the four white robed men that looked awful in their sterile white cloth robes that meant they were from the Rex's personal university on Earth. These men were probably the most indoctrinated people in the Imperium into the cult of the Rex's lies, deceit and corruption.

She couldn't allow these people to do anything against her, her library or any of the thousands of people on all the floors. She had to protect them.

The sweet aromas of pine, cherry and apples filled Aria's senses leaving the wonderful taste of warm apple pie on her tongue just like how her mother had baked when she was a child. Her mother would have hated what the Rex had done to history.

"Yes, what can I do for you fine gentleman?" Aria asked.

Aria noticed that she couldn't see any of the men's faces. It was like they were shrouded in a form of shadow that wasn't dark nor light.

"We are seeking a book called the Enlighted Bible," one of the men said.

Aria slowly nodded making it seem like she was searching her memories. Of course she knew exactly what book they were referring to, it was her favourite purchase this year, a book confirming the existence of a breakaway democratic republic of humans away from the Rex's control.

That was an amazing find so she couldn't allow these stupid men to find the book and destroy it.

"That book is a danger to the safety of the Imperium," another man said. "That book contains knowledge that has the potential to shake the Imperium to its core and cause a civil war,"

Aria seriously doubted that because she had read the first few pages (more than enough to get her killed) and the book was just describing a life of freedom, learning and pleasure in the solar systems controlled by the Enlightened Republic.

"I do not know of this book," Aria said, knowing she was done for.

Aria looked around in some vain hope of trying to find an escape path or something but there wasn't one. She knew every single inch of this library and there was no escape. She already had a feeling there were more white robed men on other floors just waiting for her to escape.

And those men would kill her.

"I just wanted to learn about the past, learning is not a crime," Aria said.

The men laughed and the tallest of the men stepped forward and arrested Aria, handcuffing her with holographic cuffs.

"Aria Pinncock you are an Enemy of The True History of Humanity and you are a terrorist trying to spread lies and corruption about the Great Rex," he said.

Aria just laughed as the men led her away and she quickly realised that she had to escape no matter what because these men would interrogate her to find the book.

But once they had the book they would kill her.

***

The awful aromas of burnt petrol, ozone and death filled Aria's senses as she leant against the icy cold black metal wall of the interrogation chamber. She was half expecting something grander considering these people were most probably the top-secret organisation known as the *Erasers*.

But the interrogation chamber was nothing more than a black metal box without a table or chair or very good environmental systems it turned out. It was just all rather uncreative but she supposed that was the point.

She, like everyone else in the Imperium, knew that if someone was picked up by the Erasers then they really were as good as dead and the Erasers on the interrogation ship were in constant communication with the ground force. So sooner or later the book would be found by the ground force and whoever came to interrogate her would kill her.

And it was even worse that the interrogations always happened on a big bulky circular ship that always struck fear in the hearts of humans whenever they saw it. Aria really hated it how she was now on one of those damn ships.

Aria had no idea whatsoever if she had done enough to hide the book. All she actually wanted was to finish reading it, learning about it and developing her knowledge about what the galaxy was really like instead of what the Rex wanted her to believe.

"Do not attack," a female computerised voice said.

Aria stood up perfectly straight as the deafening roar of a faulty teleportation hummed around the chamber.

A moment later a very tall white robed woman appeared, she looked the same as the men but her boots were black and she actually had her hood up.

And Aria couldn't help but feel like she was hearing a strange sound in the background but she couldn't quite identify what it was.

"You are currently listening to psycho-conditioning files making you more likely to tell me the location of the book," the woman said coldly. "You are a terrorist and you will die but how quickly and painfully is down to you,"

Aria just couldn't understand how the hell the Imperium had actually gotten like this, it was just impossible to imagine how an Imperium that loved, treasured and worshipped learning and history had gone so backwards so quickly.

"I will not allow you to destroy knowledge," Aria said.

The woman laughed. "Knowledge is nothing more than a weapon. Whoever controls knowledge controls people. The Rex controls knowledge so he controls every human in the Imperium and he basically controls the Keres too,"

Aria bit her lip at the sheer mention of alien Keres. A poor innocent alien race with beautiful magic that the Rex had decided were a threat so he bullied them into a war and submission and crippled a peaceful race.

Aria hated it when she had learnt the truth about the Keres, but sadly that history book had been burnt by a "friend" of hers. She was so glad she pushed him through an airlock, by accident of course.

"I will ask you three times a simple question and if you do not tell me after the third question I will kill you using crippling pain. Where is the book?"

Aria looked around. She had barely any time to free herself and she really had no intention of dying today.

Her former husband that died a few years ago fighting the Keres in the futile war would have wanted her to go out and find love again. And her mother would want her to protect history.

"Okay then you are refusing to answer me," the woman said.

Aria focused on the seams of the interrogation chamber but the damn workmanship was so fine that the entire chamber seemed to be moulded from a single sheet of steel.

There were no weak points.

Aria stood up and started tapping the walls.

"You will not find anything. Where is the book?"

Aria frowned. She really was running out of time to escape and then she realised that she was a history professor first and foremost regardless of whatever the Rex said.

Two hundred years ago when the Erasers were first founded, Aria read an article and interview written by an escapee before she was brutally burnt alive but she wrote that no one watched the interrogations and the only people who could escape were the interrogators.

That was what Aria needed to focus on. And because the woman had teleported in, she had to have a teleporter on her.

Aria just looked at the woman and smiled. The woman seemed to shudder.

Aria went over to the woman and placed her hands around her neck. The woman didn't seem to react but Aria pulled her hood down. Revealing the woman had a cybernetic eye so someone was watching her.

"You read the interview too then," the woman said. "I was like you once but no one escapes this place,"

Aria spat at the woman as she realised the so-called escapee was just a trap to lure idiots like her to their deaths. But her plan was still going to work.

Aria punched the woman, smashing her eye so no one else was watching them and she knew she only had moments left before someone checked on her.

Aria quickly changed clothes with the woman and made sure that the hood was up on her and the woman interrogator was dressed in her clothes.

A moment later three large black armoured humans appeared and Aria just looked at them with such a fierce aura of authority that the men actually bowed at her.

Aria really loved the technology that shrouded her face from the men's glare.

"She is dead. Let us leave," Aria said.

The men nodded and the deafening roar of a faulty teleportation filled the air and Aria just smiled as she teleported away and now she just needed to escape this ship before her deception was found out.

***

A few hours later, Aria crawled up into a small little ball inside the large(ish) bright white pod of a space shuttle that she had stolen from the Eraser Ship. She had tried to disable the tracker, the autopilot and all the rest of the annoying things that the Imperium installed on their shuttles and ships to make sure people like her didn't steal them, but she wasn't sure.

She had been flying for about an hour and the circular Eraser Ship didn't seem to be tracking her or anything so it seemed to be okay for now. Aria just wanted to get away from the Imperium, the Rex's forces and actually just wanted freedom.

The pod shuttle was thankfully simple and it wasn't too hard to figure out it worked with only a few bright white holograms forming her commands for her.

She had already worked out how to make the shuttle speed up, slow down and turn a little so hopefully that was everything she really needed to know for the moment. The pod also had some great environmental systems with the sweet senses of apple pie, pecans and oranges filling the air and after being interrogated it was such a relaxing smell.

As Aria watched the pitch darkness of space slowly go past her with bright white stars in the distance and a handful of planets from her home system going past, Aria just smiled because she might have been a criminal now and an enemy of the Rex's true history, but she was free.

Freedom was a myth in the Imperium and now Aria could finally go out and seek the amazing Enlightened Republic. She would live there, get to taste their way of life and most importantly she would get to learn what history was actually like.

Because the Rex could always try to take the girl out of history, but it was impossible to take the history out of the girl. And that was why she loved being an enemy of history.

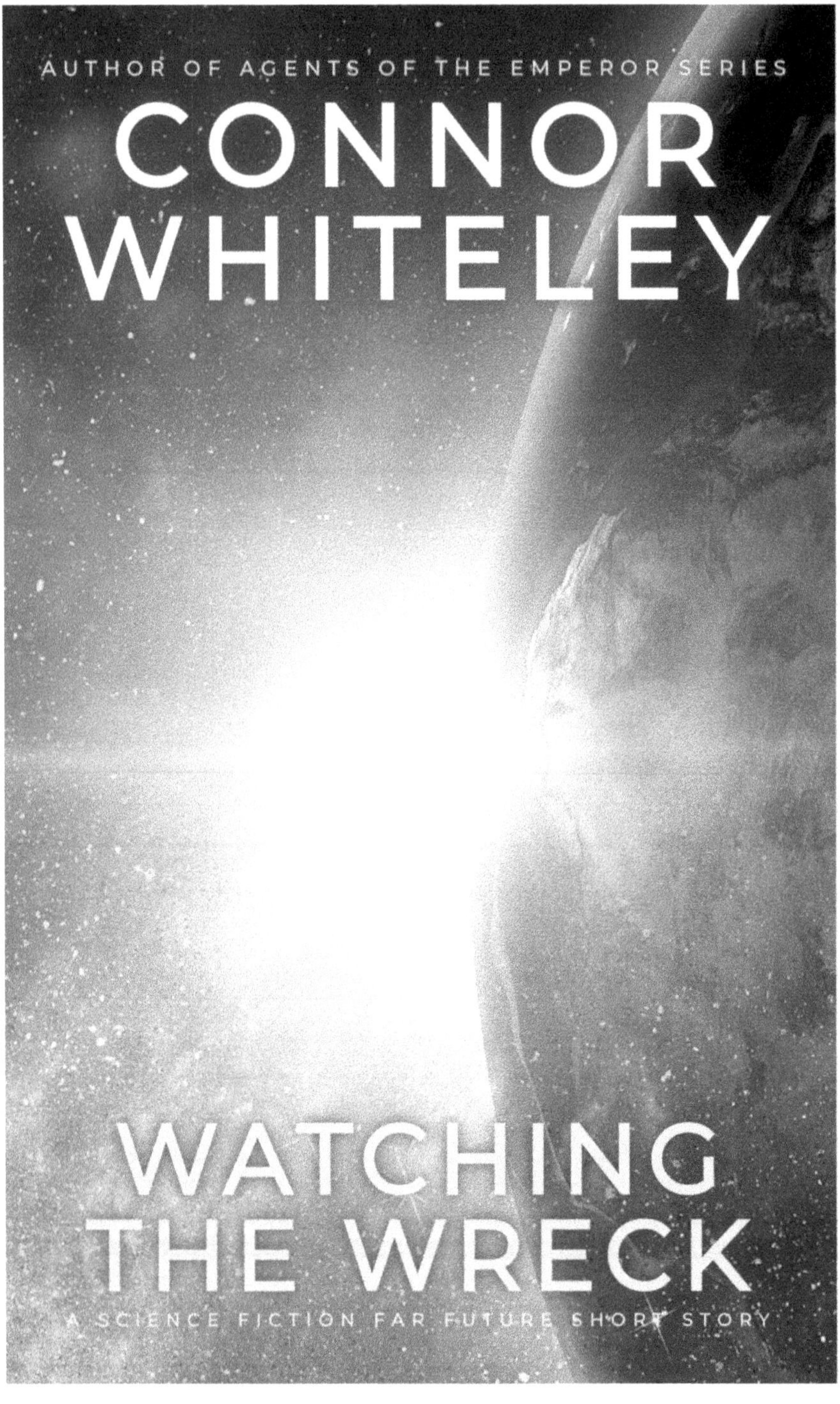
AUTHOR OF AGENTS OF THE EMPEROR SERIES
CONNOR WHITELEY
WATCHING THE WRECK
A SCIENCE FICTION FAR FUTURE SHORT STORY

WATCHING THE WRECK

When I, Mila Scott, was younger I actually loved going into the cold, darkness of space with my brothers and sisters flying about in our junker of a space shuttle. An awful little pod-like object that I was always scared of it falling apart, that was exactly how old it was. Me and my sisters and brothers saw some wonderful things in the Imperium, massive stars, circular battleships and little bright white pods that tried to kill us once or twice.

Those really were the days of our youth that I absolutely loved. Then as we all grew older, a little fatter and not a lot wiser, we all went our separate and rather different ways.

My three brothers they joined the Imperial Army and all died during the stupid war with the peaceful aliens known as the Keres, all because our stupid leader the Rex was scared of their magic. They all died.

My sisters went to study medicine on Earth, a so-called great honour but because both of them were certainly daughters of our mother, they questioned way too much and I think the Erasers killed them so others wouldn't question the Rex's version of events.

That's the silly galaxy we live in.

And as for little old me, well I was stupid enough to study history and become a history graduate, I even have a PhD in Early Imperium Studies and the Rex hates that subject.

That's why I'm sitting pretty at my bright white metal desk inside my even whiter cubicle with its awfully smooth walls that I hate, and

I'm having to stare at a little holographic computer screen.

Thankfully, there's a small red dot flashing at the very, very edge of my computer screen but until it gets closer towards the centre of my screen, I really don't want to do anything about it.

Personally I just want to add some holo-art of something to the perfectly smooth walls but I cannot. Apparently that would endanger my life, it's rubbish of course but I always like to see their excuses for controlling every single aspect of my life.

The cubicle itself isn't so bad I suppose, there's a brand-new small single bed that is rather comfortable, it just sits behind me during the day and it doubles as a sofa and dining table. The people in charge here don't exactly give you much.

Granted, I hate its soft blue sheets because I could have sworn the bosses here coat the material in a waxy substance that annoys me when I go to sleep. I also flat out the little food shoot, that really is nothing more than a metal pipe that drops food into my cubicle.

I mean I am no dog, cat or animal so why can't I just get given food like every other normal person in the Imperium. Normally food is just shipped to entire planets from Farming Worlds but clearly that might not happen here.

And the smell is just the worse at feeding time, because the pipe connects directly outside the cubicle gets filled with the disgusting senses of burnt ozone, petrol and raw meat. It flat out isn't a nice place, I hate it.

"Three minutes until Exercise Time," a loud computerised voice said.

Oh yes, if you can believe it. The bosses here actually give us very set exercise time, it's basically the only ten minutes we're allowed to leave these cubicles each day. And that's why I'm so excited about when I can finally leave this form of prison.

Officially, when the Rex decided to outlaw history (because it was the only thing that could challenge his lies), he arrested, killed and captured all the history professionals in the Imperium. I was one of the "Lucky" few that got to enlist in the army and now I am stuck on this awful military moon just watching the border between the Imperium and the dying Keres Empire.

In other words, I get to stare at pitch darkness all day.

And my mother said studying history was a brilliant idea.

The wonderful sounds of my friends (my other inmates) laughing, talking and discussing what they're found on their computer screens is loud enough to get through the thick white walls, and I'm so looking forward to seeing them.

Even ten minutes with them is a wonderful distraction to the mind numbing pain of this prison.

I get up and past my bed where the wall should dissolve and I should be able to go outside.

"Not for you. You have an object on your screen. You must sort it out first before going for your exercise time, no extra time will be given," the computerised voice said.

I wanted to smash my fists into a wall or something. How dare this stupid voice and my bosses deduct my exercise time from me just because of some dumb red spot.

I went back over to my computer screen and tapped my fingers on the spot.

I read the output as the tapping always gave me a light reading and scan of whatever the object was. It was certainly Imperium in nature, I would recognise the black circular design anywhere.

But the materials were all wrong, and my knowledge of history and my wonderful relationship with a boy studying Military History (he was one that got a bullet in the head by the Rex), I knew these materials haven't been used in two thousand years to build Imperium ships.

I zoom in even more because I just couldn't understand this, this ship is coming in the direction of the Keres Empire and yet this is an Imperium vessel.

The Keres Empire have always, always been peaceful, magical and great aliens that truly respect humanity, well unlike humanity determined to slaughter them, and even the most extreme elements of Keres society (that only came about because of the war) would never keep an Imperium vessel and then return it later on.

That was a very human thing to do.

"Computer," I said, "I need access to the others,"

"Access denied. You are a Level 5 Operative, you do not need lessers to help you," the voice said.

Damn it. I seriously hated my bosses, and part of the problem was that I actually was that good unfortunately so the bosses trusted me. I had sadly stopped a number of smuggling ships trying to bring Keres refugees into Imperial space so they could get food, medical supplies and clean water for their people.

All things that the Imperium had stolen from them after the war.

I zoomed in and really focused on the circular ship and I started to scan it deeply. I had to know what was going on here.

The ship had no power, no engines, no weapon systems. All of it had been taken out and that actually was a rather Keres thing to do because it helped them to maintain the peace, but there were also no bodies.

Typically, and the Rex would never admit this, the Keres always used their magic to knock out the human attackers so they could enter a peaceful sleep and then the Keres would return the attackers to the Imperium.

That was partly why they lost the war. Their commitment to peace was amazing if not their downfall.

Then a single reading popped up and I just smiled. It turned out there was a single corpse on the ship and it proved everything I ever wanted to do about the ship.

There was an Imperial corpse on the ship, meaning a murder had taken place and if there was one thing my bosses hated it was a dead body.

Now I just needed to play it to my advantage.

I just hoped that the computer and my bosses had forgotten how me and my friends were all excellent coders and we could easily manipulate a hologram system to scan for whatever we want. It was amazing the skills you could pick up.

I could easily do this work on my own but I just wanted to see my friends and most importantly I wanted to see if there was a chance of escape.

I didn't want to be stuck on this damn moon anymore.

"Computer, I need access to the others now. There's a dead human on that ship and if killers are onboard then we have to know before it reaches Imperial Space," I said, hoping beyond hope it would work.

There was a long pause.

"Granted. Doors will open now and everyone will meet in the Command Centre," the voice said.

I weakly smiled, not only because I was going to get a chance to see my friends but also because the Command Centre was where our captors or "bosses" were. And I had always known some of my friends wanted their freedom.

Maybe this was the time to fight for our freedom too.

***

Now granted, I have never been to the command centre before but I would have imagined it was a little more high-tech than this junk.

I was standing in nothing more than a large dirty white cubicle about four times bigger than my own cubicle, so it was still rather small. There were barely any holograms, and the only white holograms there were were about the weather, not something I'm very interested in knowing about on a moon.

There was a small porthole that was just showed how the bright orange rock of the moon stretched on endlessly with craters, unexploded bombs and our cubicles punctuating the orange rock.

It was not pretty.

Thankfully, there was a huge holographic table in the middle of the command centre showing a large flickering depiction of the black circular wreck I had found earlier.

And all my friends were here, which was amazing.

There were only five other people here out of ten, so I was a little worried about where they were but I didn't mind.

My best friend in the entire galaxy, Paula was standing next to me in her normal pink jeans, hoody and boots. She was more than ready to work.

"This is a wreck from two centuries before the Keres War," a man called Andy said, sporting a very dirty jacket that looked like it was about to fall apart at any moment.

"But how did it end up behind Keres lines?" Paula said.

"Well I don't know what we can say without getting killed," James said, a very short man.

I smiled because that was the truth of it. We could all easily solve this mystery if we were allowed to discuss history but of course that would only get us all killed.

And I really didn't like the gentle humming of the command centre, almost like our bosses were preparing to gas us all at a moment's notice.

"Wait, so we all know if we don't solve this mystery with the wreck, we don't get fed tonight but could this be an opportunity?" I said.

Well, if our bosses were going to gas us anyway, I at least wanted to know if the others wanted freedom.

"From what I remember, the Imperium has always used the other basic communication network," Andy said.

I nodded as I swiped the holographic table a few times and tried to establish a connection with the wreck. Then I remembered how it didn't have any power.

The holographic table flashed and a small warning hologram came up. It was saying the scan had just been scanned by a magical sign.

"There's Keres on that ship," Paula said, failing to show her excitement.

I didn't want to comment as I heard the command centre humming even louder and the others were starting to show their own concern at the sound.

If I wanted to make sure me and my friends survived this then I had to be very careful here. The problem was that this command centre was set to kill us so we could never escape and pass on our historical knowledge to anyone else. Including the Keres.

Another problem was that the Keres were sending a wreckage towards us and I don't know why.

And to make things even worse, my friends were building their assumption on the Keres were here to save us. What if they weren't?

But as the humming of the command centre reached a deafening level, I just knew I couldn't wait around for answers. We needed to escape now, ideally find our bosses and kill them.

"Cannons activating," a computerised voice said.

"Damn it," I said.

Our bosses were preparing to destroy the wreckage so the Keres died and we couldn't escape. Damn them. Damn the Rex. Damn the Imperium.

As one me and my friends all started typing on the holographic table and tried to access the moon's central mainframe so we could access all computer systems on the moon.

"I did it," Paula said.

I moved round to her set of holograms. I was the best coder amongst all of us so I took control.

Our bosses were fighting us and trying to force us out but they were thinking I was going after the cannons.

I wasn't.

Our bosses kicked out everyone else from the system but I was here logged in. I was going after the gas and environmental systems that would ultimately kill us.

I found them. Then I programmed the environmental systems to pump the toxic gas into the chamber where my bosses were.

The system complied and the loud deafening screams of my bosses echoed around the command centre as I played the audio from their chamber beneath us.

My friends laughed, hugged each other and I loved their sheer happiness but I had to save the Keres. The cannons were still being activated and then the results of a much better scan came in that Andy had started running in secret.

There were thousands of Keres refugees on the ship that had been using their magic to shield themselves from scanning. And in fact the entire wreckage wasn't Imperial in nature, it was a beautifully, bejewelled stunning Keres battleship.

I had to save those innocent people.

I found the cannons. They were about to fire.

I hit the kill code but it didn't work.

I tried changing the target.

It didn't work.

So I tried to kill the power.

All the power on the moon deactivated and everything went perfectly silent and it was only in the sheer deadly silence of the moon that I realised just how much background noise I had tuned out since I got here.

But that included the environmental systems were off too.

And it wasn't like I could reactivate the power because the cannon commands were still in the computer system waiting to be carried out the moment there was power again.

I just looked at all my amazing friends, Paula, Andy and the rest. They all looked so shocked but they were smiling.

Not because they were happy about dying on some moon that they hated, but because they were going to sacrifice themselves so innocent people could live.

I was damn proud of them.

My lungs jerked as I tried to breathe in air that wasn't there and then my lungs burnt painfully as they screamed out for air. Air that was never coming for them.

I was about to shut my eyes and allow the darkness of death to claim me when I felt a warm magical energy wrap around me and my vision was blinded by a beautiful golden light.

***

When I opened my eyes again, I couldn’t exactly understand why I was laying down on something hard, light blue and oddly warm but it was nice, so much nicer than anything human I had ever felt.

I pushed myself and allowed my legs to dangle over the edge, and I was pleased that it was a sort of medical table that I had been sitting on. It looked like it was made from a yellow sort of plastic but the Keres were always masters of technology and making things. This was probably a material I had never thought of before.

The medical chamber itself was stylish and like a massive pod with beautiful baby blue walls with the artist's brush marks swirling, twirling and whirling around each other. It was so beautiful to look at and even the jewelled ceiling with diamonds, rubies and stranger, more alien gems was simply stunning.

The quiet humming, laughing and talking of my best friends gave me such relief. At least they were alive, well and seemingly very happy so at least I didn’t get everyone killed, and it was only now that I was realising exactly what we had done.

We had saved so many innocent people from dying a painful death, we had finally escaped our bosses and that damn moon so now the Imperium could no longer watch their precious border with the Keres Empire in case an invasion even happened.

But it wouldn’t and I was okay with that because me and my friends were free.

The sweet smells of oranges, jasmine and lemons filled the air as a section of the wall dissolved and in came a very thin and male Keres. He was humanoid in shape and features but he was much tall, almost dangerously thin and he certainly looked a lot more regal than humans ever could.

“Thank you,” the male Keres said bowing elegantly.

“No, thank you for saving us. You can drop us off wherever, me and my friends don’t want to burden you,”

The Keres laughed so beautifully that it was like listening to a melody. “Now it seems you are being silly because your crew have already accepted an offer of employment, and I hope you will accept it too. Live with us and join us and become one of us or yes, we will drop you off whenever you desire,"

If this person wasn't Keres then I naturally would have denied it because this was a very dangerous offer. But I am a history professor and Doctor of History, I know that the Keres are deeply caring, supportive and protective people and they will always see me and my crew as one of them.

If we live with the Keres then we will never be in danger from them, they will live freely and we can actually experience joy once more. And I want that so badly.

"I accept," I said bowing to the Keres as that was their equivalent of a handshake.

"Excellent, your friends are in the dining chamber playing, I think you call it, carks?"

Because he was being so nice to me, my friends and he had offered us freedom and joy after a lifetime of pain, I didn't care to correct him. But as I left the medical chamber, I was looking forward to playing *cards*, starting my new life and finally start watching the Imperium from the other side and I have to admit it really will be like watching a wreckage that would never enslave me again.

Because I wouldn't let it.

AUTHOR OF AGENTS OF THE EMPEROR SERIES
CONNOR WHITELEY
POWDERY MILDEW INVASION
A SCIENCE FICTION FAR FUTURE SHORT STORY

POWDERY MILDEW INVASION

Doctor Tarcey Gibson absolutely loved the stunning, beautiful fiery sun start to set in the distance as its intense orange rays lit up the sky like an intense inferno, and she could have sworn even the planet of Farmicus 3 was roaring in protest of the intense sunset.

She couldn't deny that was one of the most stunning things about the entire planet. And Tarcey loved watching the sunset over the rolling fields of grape vines that stretched on for miles upon miles over the rolling, sweeping hills of the central regions.

The massive black grapes the size of her head shone brightly in the setting sun and Tarcey just couldn't deny how perfectly seductive they looked. She had worked on tens of different worlds in the Enlightened Republic since she fled the oppression and cruelty of the Imperium and she had never had the pleasure of seeing grapes as large and as perfect as these ones.

She enjoyed staring out at the perfectly straight lines of immense head-sized vines as they blew softly in the warm roaring wind that was slowly starting to turn cooler and cooler as the evening temperature dropped.

The hairs on her neck slowly rose like soldiers and Tarcey just smiled. The air was sweet with the wonderful hints of jasmine, grapes and wine from the nearest wineries that almost popped up like trees on the planet. It was just perfect here and Tarcey couldn't ask for a better life, watching, maintaining and continuing to learn about these almost magical plants.

All around Tarcey were nothing but endless fields of vineyards but she hated the real reason why she was out here. She enjoyed the sheer contrast between the beautiful vines and the sheer bright orange sand and soil that made up the planet's outer crust.

It was a strange combination of two colour extremes.

Tarcey forced herself to tear her eyes off the breathtaking setting sun and she focused on the large pointy leaves of the vines. She knew they should have been long, dark green with points like knives but that wasn't what these vines had at all.

She hated how a thick coating of white powder had covered each and every leaf on the vines. It was powdery mildew, a horrible fungi, that attacked and killed the plants its corrupting touch invaded and it eventually killed the plants.

Tarcey really didn't like how the white powder was no longer just coating the leaves but infecting the thick, strong stems of the vines that were as thick as Tarcey's arms.

The vines were meant to swirl, twirl and whirl around the huge holographic canes to support the perfect structure for the vines as they grew. But now the vines were deadly white and with each blow of the awful wind, millions of tiny white pores poured off the vines.

Allowing the infection to spread.

Tarcey hated how nothing seemed to be working to stop the invasion of the powdery mildew. She had tried all the standard tips and tricks that she had been taught at university.

She had tried chemical, both domestic and military-grade anti-fungi, she had tried organic methods using milk because milk was a natural anti-fungi solution but nothing was working.

And that was seriously starting to annoy her now.

Tarcey just watched in utter horror as a massive gust of warm wind blew past her creating an immense white cloud of fungi pores to blow off into the air and fly towards more crops.

She had no idea how the hell the mildew had been allowed to come to the planet in the first place. It was her job to make sure all the local fungi and bacteria and viruses were dealt with quickly.

Tarcey had checked and double-checked every single ship, person and cargo cruiser that came into the planet's single spaceport and no one had powdery mildew on them.

This fungi shouldn't have been on the planet but somehow it was and somehow it was destroying the vines.

And as much as Tarcey didn't want to admit it, those amazing months of dating a sexy turncoat military commander (later assassinated by the Imperium of course) had taught her to focus on the bigger picture and that scared her a hell of a lot more than she ever wanted to admit.

The Enlightened Republic only had access to entire planets dedicated to food production and because it was only a small group of breakaway systems every single farming world had a critical function to serve.

If this planet failed then billions of innocent lives would be impacted and Tarcey hated to admit it, but billions of people might starve to death.

She knew the grapes weren't only used for wine but for cereal, meat replacement and in almost every dish the Republic served. These grapes were perfect.

The Republic couldn't afford to lose this planet.

Tarcey took out a very small black-box device that she held in her hand and she turned it on, revealing a large red hologram showing a whole bunch of empirical tests that she was running on the air.

The air was perfectly normal. Tarcey was more than happy about that, at least she didn't need a rebreather or something she couldn't afford right now.

She brushed the device against one of the white powdery leaves and the device burst into flames.

Tarcey threw it on the ground and stomped it out.

She had no idea what caused it but now she was even more determined to go back to the lab and find the truth.

She had lives to save and she wasn't letting anyone stop her.

***

Tarcey was so excited as she went into her large sterile white lab inside a constantly moving and swirling sphere in the heart of the capital winery two hundred kilometres away. Tarcey just stopped in the doorway and was so happy to be back in her real home.

The lab hummed to life and Tarcey smiled as the pretty red, blue and orange lights danced up the white walls smiling at her. She had always loved the Chief Engineer developing those mini-artificial intelligence beings for her.

The sterile white floor in the shape of honeycomb pulsed and flashed a couple of times for her, and Tarcey couldn't believe it had been so long since she had been in the lab. Everyone was so happy to see her and she really enjoyed the bitter-sweet aroma of intense coffee, sweet vanilla and jasmine that clung to the air leaving the great taste of coffee cake form on her tongue.

Tarcey went into the lab and she could feel all the energy, heartache and concern she had built up her over the course of her searching and surveying of the fields were melted away.

This was her lab and she was finally going to get some answers to whatever the hell was going on. If this was a simple case of a natural fungi getting out of control then she knew she could easily find some options, but she doubted it was going to be that simple.

Something had destroyed her scanner and that was something concerning. Nothing she had ever investigated before had damaged her equipment. Some of the pathogens she dealt with had made her go to hospital for a few weeks but her equipment was always fine.

This time she was okay, it was her equipment that died.

As soon as Tarcey got to the middle of the lab, a large baby blue hologram appeared of Tarcey's old lab assistant, Dexter Clarke. She still missed him, he was a great man and Tarcey really did owe him everything. If he hadn't sacrificed himself then her and a group of innocent children never could have fled into the Enlightened Republic.

He was a great man. Tarcey had to solve this mystery to honour him.

Tarcey looked at the cute hologram of Dex as it materialised, showing his strong jawline, slim body and long brown hair that he always refused to cut unless it was the first day of a brand-new year. He never had explained why he did that but Tarcey didn't mind. It was just a little quirk she loved about him.

"Doctor," Dex said, "I am detecting increasing in the Powdery Mildew issue. I have detected it spreading strongly into the Northern and Southern regions,"

"Damn," Tarcey said.

She just couldn't believe how quickly this problem was spreading. The Republic could survive (barely) if the grapes in the central regions were destroyed but if the wheat fields in the North and the fruits and vegetables of the South were annihilated then the Republic was in massive trouble.

Tarcey doubted the other planets could easily pick up the slack.

"Dex," Tarcey said, "my scanner, did it send you any data before its destruction?"

"Partial data transfer was successful," Dex said.

Tarcey supposed that was good. There was some data to play with but Tarcey really wanted a complete dataset so she could really start to understand exactly what she was facing.

So far getting that sample was proving impossible and from panic messages from other scientists all over the planet they were having just as much luck.

"Bring up the data so far," Tarcey said. "And run a comparison between the fungi samples of powdery mildew on other planets with our data,"

Dex nodded and clicked his fingers. Tarcey watched as the partial cell reconstruction and plant DNA appeared next to him. It wasn't much to go on and Tarcey might have been a good student but even she knew her limits.

This data was meaningless.

"Doctor, there is not enough data for an intergalactic

comparison,"

Tarcey nodded. That was to be expected and as much as she hated this problem, she was starting to panic a lot more than she wanted to admit.

So many lives were depending on her, and her alone.

"Dex, in the data transfer, did the scanner give an explanation for its destruction?"

"Of course Doctor," Dex said. "The scanner was told to self-destruct. Something in the sample you were scanning managed to override all Republic safety codes,"

Tarcey was flat out amazed someone could actually do that. She had heard of plenty of really, really smart computer and electronic people fleeing the Imperium but to actually imagine they would destroy the safety codes of the Republic was amazing.

They weren't dealing with a natural form of the fungi.

"Are there any biological weapon programmes currently operating in the Republic or Imperium?" Tarcey asked.

"That information is not accessible to empirical staff. Only military commanders and personnel have access to the desired information,"

"Of course they do," Tarcey said. She hated it when the damn military interfered with her investigations.

"I would send a request,"

"Do it, Alpha Priority," Tarcey said. "Code Plague Grape,"

Tarcey had no doubt if anyone knew about the ancient code words that the Republic were founded on as a method of secret communication but she couldn't rest the fate of the Republic on another person's memory.

If she did that then humanity was doomed.

"What about the data from the other scientists?" Tarcey asked. "Presumably I am not the only person to try to get a data sample,"

"All are currently incomplete with not enough data points to run a comparison," Dex said.

"I know," Tarcey said smiling, "but what if you put them all together? What if you fit every line of code and data together like a jigsaw of ancient earth?"

Tarcey watched Dex play with his long brown hair for a moment and he nodded.

A moment later Tarcey just grinned as she watched the holographic strands of DNA get longer and longer. She saw the different genes, chromosomes and proteins swirl, twirl and whirl together to create exactly what she wanted.

She was an expert in plant biology and she knew instantly that a lot of these biological links were impossible and they most certainly were not found in nature.

As the fungi sample grew and grew as Tarcey noticed that nanobots were swimming around inside the cells of the fungi sample, she realised she had seen and actually studied this exact DNA modifier before.

This was most certainly Imperial genetic engineering and biological warfare.

She had no idea how an Imperial agent had smuggled this weapon into the Republic let alone onto her most holy of worlds, but she now knew exactly how it worked.

Now she only needed to find out how to stop it.

"The nanobots," Tarcey said. "Run a deconstruction scan on them,"

Dex nodded and with a swirl of a hand, Tarcey grinned like a kid in a candy store as she studied the lines upon lines of code showing the instructions, signals and more that the nanobots were programmed to do.

Dex had already disabled a lot of the defence systems that would have destroyed her lab in a heartbeat. Tarcey had to admit that Dex was incredible and the person who designed these nanobots were amazing.

Tarcey read her line and was impressed that each nanobot was programmed to tell the fungi cell to spread and spread more and more rapidly with each passing day.

The reproduction rate of the fungi cells were over a thousand times faster than normal powdery mildew cells. Tarcey was scared as hell about its effectiveness but there were weaknesses here.

And Tarcey had graduated top of her class and she knew exactly how to use this weapon against itself.

"Listen to me carefully," Tarcey said to Dex grinning, "and reprogramme these nanobots exactly how I tell you to. We have a planet to save,"

***

Tarcey was so damn happy a week later as she walked along the bright orange sand and soil in amongst immensely tall grapevines that were easily ten times taller than her.

Each vine had leaves the size of houses, stems as thick as city blocks and grapes the size of small villages. It was so amazing and Tarcey had loved every single minute of the project, and she actually didn't mind not being able to see the stunning sunset as she explored the fields that were once much smaller.

Tarcey stopped and ran her fingers across the huge warm leaves that barely moved against her hand. Everything was so much bigger that she supposed the plant barely felt it. And Tarcey was so happy that the dark vibrant green of the vines were now strong and there wasn't a single hint of white powder on any plant on the entire planet.

Tarcey had later explained it to her bosses and the amazing Supreme General Abbie, the leader of the Republic, as a simple job of reprogramming the nanobots to instead of attacking the vines, they needed to attack the other fungi cells and encourage the bines to grow.

She had no idea it was going to work so well.

And once the entire planet unleashed the reprogramming signal that all the nanobots received, they immediately started encouraging more growth.

Tarcey had to admit it was a nightmare for the first day because the water and fertiliser drones were going so hard, half of them broke from overuse.

Another very fun challenge Tarcey had loved solving.

Tarcey just enjoyed the sweet intense aroma of the black grapes around her as she looked forward to the bright future of the Republic. Their food supply was safe, the military had confirmed the Imperium was working on biological weapons and that base was now annihilated and everyone was excited about the increased production.

Meaning no matter how many great Enlightened people who wanted to embrace democracy and freedom found their way to the Republic, they would always be safe, fed and happy in these little systems of paradise.

Exactly what Tarcey had always wanted and she was never ever going to stop protecting that most precious idea, and having a lot of fun along the way.

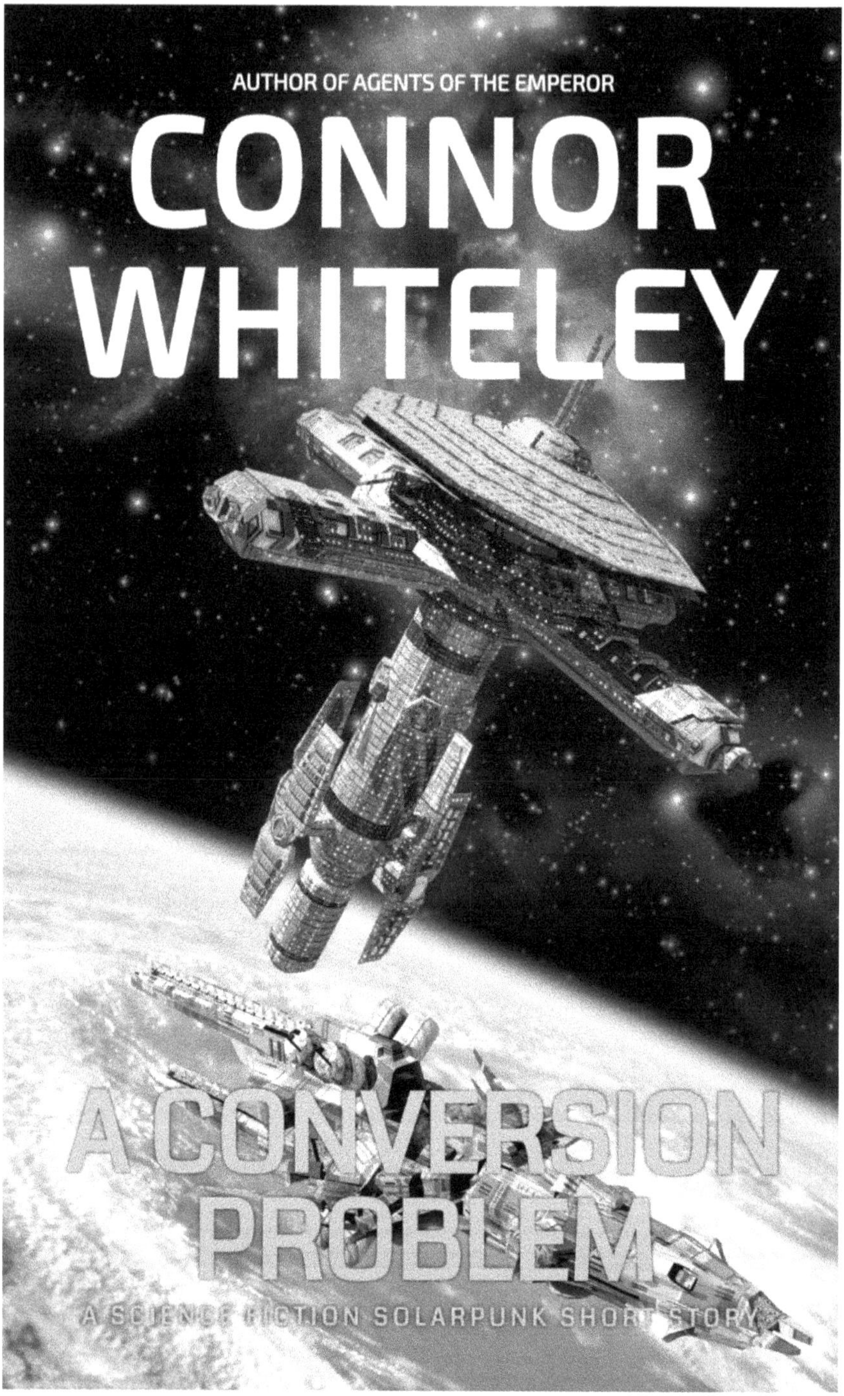
AUTHOR OF AGENTS OF THE EMPEROR
CONNOR
WHITELEY
A CONVERSION
PROBLEM
A SCIENCE FICTION SOLARPUNK SHORT STORY

A CONVERSION PROBLEM

Chief Scientist Sofia Walsh absolutely loved her amazing new job working at a conversion centre where all of humanity's amazing waste was converted into food and energy and water for humanity to consume and enjoy without harming any planet or ecosystem in the Empire. It was simply brilliant and a job she absolutely loved.

Sofia leant against the icy cold metal railings on the silver metal balcony she was standing on that overlooked her impressive dominion of the Conversion Centre. Sofia really loved the immensely massive rectangular room that was two kilometres high and another five kilometres wide, when she had first heard of this conversion centre she hadn't understood why it all needed to be so massive, but that was the benefit of being on a large blue blade-like cruiser in high orbit of a planet.

Building the conversion centre in space meant that it was so much easier to build and they weren't restricted on size whatsoever, so it was only logical in a way that they had tried to build the centre in orbit instead of on a planet on a much smaller scale.

The smooth grey walls of the conversion centre was something that Sofia definitely wanted to change in time, the walls sort of made the centre feel icy cold and scary and sad in a way, so Sofia was just waiting for her boss's boss to approve her ideas for changing the walls to bright green or blue or basically any colour that would add a touch of warmth to the place.

Because considering Sofia had been born on Earth, she was used to warmth and crisp clean air that stunk of pine, refreshing and damp that the conversion centre definitely didn't smell it. It wasn't a bad smell per se but Sofia really wished the ship's cleaning systems would at least add some scents to the air to get rid of aroma of sweat, testosterone and other unpleasant things from the workers.

As the conversion centre started to sound of banging, pumping and bubbling, Sofia focused on the rows upon rows of immensely impressive machines down below her.

Sofia seriously loved the amazing great-looking grey metal cylinders that stretched the entire length of the conversion centre and whilst they did only look like cylinders, Sofia was surprised at the sheer amount of skill and technological marvels inside each one.

As every single cylinder in the conversion centre managed to get food, human and animal waste teleported into it from all the blade-like ships and shuttles in the system, from all the planets and basically whenever there was waste that needed to be dealt with.

Sofia just focused on how smooth and shiny and impressive each of the cylinders looked as they set to work like they weren't even struggling.

It was just amazing to Sofia how every single solar system and the vast majority of ships in the Empire had some kind of conversion centre onboard just like this, but different sizes and scales depending on the size of the ship of course, because it really meant that humanity rarely needed to do mining and other awful harmful activity that destroyed planets, ecosystems and natural wonders.

Sofia had first really gotten into the field and learnt about the conversion centres after a private company had landed on a luxurious ocean world that had stunning mountains, beaches and islands that she had been holidaying on when she was a teenager, and the private company simply started mining on the world.

It was even worst when they started pouring their waste products into the oceans, killing off all ocean life and Sofia just knew she would never ever forget seeing all those dead fish, whales and alien sea life that was just floating there.

The private company had released so much waste product into the oceans that the planet was unsafe to live on, there were floods and so many people died. Sofia hated the sheer panic, uncertainty and death was spreading throughout the world as the evacuation happened.

And the very last straw that had Sofia so determined to work for the conversion centre was the simple fact that a disease had been created by the waste products so they ripped through the survivors like a tidal wave.

Sofia barely survived that holiday, and it still gave her little comfort that the private company had all been arrested and executed for breaking the Great Human Empire's strict environmental laws.

"Doctor," a man said.

Sofia smiled as she heard the smooth sexy voice of her assistant, Francis Cole, who was an amazing researcher, scientist and academic in his own right. And Sofia really did like having him around because of how helpful he was.

As he leant against the cold railings with her, Sofia had to admit he did look good in his white lab coat, black knee-high boots and large plastic eyes that he had always said his mother gave him before she died fighting some aliens on a forgotten world, and Sofia could understand that as a reason for why he didn't want to have an eye surgery like everyone else in the Empire did.

"Doctor," Francis said. "We have a problem,"

Sofia just looked at him. That was one of the weirdest things she had ever heard, she knew she was relatively new to the job of running the conversion centre but there wouldn't be a problem.

All these cylinders were state-of-the-art and Sofia had even hired double the amount of engineers in the past week, much to the dismay of her boss and his boss, just to make sure the conversion cylinders were always being serviced and perfectly okay.

"What's wrong?" Sofia asked.

Francis weakly smiled. "So you know how the teleportation transports all the waste to us?"

Sofia nodded. That was such a basic principle of the conversion centre, she would be a bit useless as the person running it all if she didn't know it.

"The teleportation link's broken on our end," Francis said.

Sofia just smiled. Not because that was funny in the slightest but more because of what it meant.

The entire conversion centre system worked on the principle that all the different ships, planets and whatever else relied on the conversion centre for waste processing simply teleported their waste to them, preventing a build-up of waste and it meant the centre would quickly and effectively deal with the waste.

If there was a delay to the processing or even worse, if there was a waste build up in the ships or wherever needed the centre for processing then Sofia actually couldn't imagine what would happen.

The Empire didn't design ships, buildings and space stations to have sanitation storage capabilities because they simply weren't needed.

So if a build-up did develop then it would only be a matter of time until there was an overflow and entire ships could get flooded with human and animal and food waste, creating an awful smell but most importantly it would be an amazing place for diseases to develop.

Sofia seriously couldn't allow that to happen.

"What do you mean?" Sofia asked.

Francis showed her a smooth black dataslate and Sofia was surprised to see the ships and planets and everywhere was still teleporting their waste to the conversion centre but the conversion centre wasn't receiving it.

It wasn't even being diverted to another conversion centre or location. It was simply not anywhere.

Sofia slowly nodded because she had heard about this teleportation theory too many times in science journals, and whilst there was no supporting evidence for it at the moment, all the scientists in the Empire were at least a little bit concerned about what it meant.

Since if matter was teleported from point A to Point B, but Point B wouldn't accept the matter and rearrange it to effectively reform whatever was teleported. Normally it would be destroyed and the corpse or whatever would rematerialize at Point B, but there was another theory.

Sofia had to admit it was crazy, but some scientists believed if Point B couldn't be reached for a teleported item then it was possible that because the teleported material existed as effectively random matter in space. It would stay like that for a time until there was so much matter in space that it had to rematerialize simply because space couldn't hold it in its teleported form anymore.

Sofia just hated to imagine the sheer chaos that would cause if it was true. Because if all the human, animal and food waste did just rematerialize randomly then it could do so anywhere. In the corridors of ships, on people's faces or even inside people.

All because no one knew where the teleported material was when it was in its teleported form that, for lack of a better term, both did and did not exist in at the same point.

Sofia just folded her arms. "I presume you've calculated how long we have until the forced waste rematerialisation happens?"

"An hour," Francis said.

Sofia just hated that, that wasn't good in the slightly and Sofia seriously hoped Francis had worked out what was causing it.

"And I have no clue what's causing it," Francis said.

Sofia smiled because they only had a single hour to effectively save the conversion centre, ships and planets from having waste rematerialise all over them.

And Sofia seriously didn't want to consider the damage that much waste would do if it wasn't stored properly.

***

Thankfully Sofia knew exactly where all the transportation links with the other planets, ships and everywhere else were controlled from, and Sofia just hoped there was an easy fix to the problem inside the Teleportation Control Room.

Which to be honest was just a very fancy name for a massive grey silver box room. Sofia had always liked its bright white walls with a hint of orange lighting that really helped to give the room a little more warmth and it even felt a little more homely compared to the main conversion centre.

But as the warmth was sadly only in the look of the place as Sofia's breath condensed into thick columns of vapour in front of her very eyes, and her skin chilled down so much little ice crystals started to form on her exposed forearms.

The temperature wasn't exactly what she wanted and she just had a little feeling that the extreme cold had something to do with the teleportation problem.

Sofia just focused on the three massive red holographic computer screens in front of her that were situated in the very centre of the silver box room. There was nothing else in the room but there was at least meant to be another person, a person who controlled and monitored the teleportation links at all times.

Sofia actually knew Christopher very well, and she seriously knew his muscles, chest and wayward parts extremely well but it was still odd that he wasn't here at his station like he was meant to be.

Sofia and Francis both looked at each other, and she was glad she wasn't the only one who found Christopher's disappearance a little strange. And with there not being any metal cupboards, filing cabinets or any sort of storage whatsoever in here, it wasn't like he was hiding.

There was literally only the three large red holographic computer screens in the silver box room, there was nothing else.

Sofia went over to the holographic computer screens but Francis gagged behind her, and Sofia realised there was a foul aroma of burnt ozone in the air.

It smelt disgusting.

"Computer," Sofia said. "Run a system's diagnostic on the teleportation links,"

Sofia probably knew that Francis had already ran such a thing but she wanted to see the results for herself, and these holographic computers in this box room were specially programmed for working the teleportation links so they might see something the other scans missed.

"What do you think caused it?" Francis asked, his cute little face shaking and chattering from the cold.

Sofia wanted to say how little she knew at the moment and that she actually needed a lot more data first, but she had known Francis a long time and like herself he was probably a little concerned if not scared.

Sofia really understood that because there was an excellent chance there was some kind of disease-ridden waste floating in the air around them or even inside of them as they spoke.

And if that did rematerialise inside of them then that would have deadly consequences.

"I suspect it's something to do with the extreme cold and smell," Sofia said. "The rest of the conversion centre and the cruiser we're on isn't being affected by the smell, cold or dropout of teleportation abilities,"

"You thinking there is something wrong with our systems only, and the systems limited to this room,"

Sofia nodded. "Definitely. Conversion Centres are designed to run on their own computer systems just in case these things happen so chances are the problem is limited and caused by our systems,"

The red holographic computers flashed a couple of times before dying completely.

Sofia just folded her arms so clearly whatever the problem was, it definitely didn't like to be scanned and now she was a lot more concerned about Christopher.

He had always been amazing at his job and it was his extreme dedication to making sure he did his job right, correct and going the extra mile that had caused Sofia and him never to date in the first place.

They were simply both too obsessed with their jobs to get into a relationship right now.

"Computer," Francis said, "are you still here?"

A popping sound echoed all over the box room like something inside the walls was being destroyed and Sofia realised that the electronics for the computers were exactly there.

Sofia went over and ran her fingers over the icy cold smoothness of the grey silver walls. She started walking around the room still with her fingers on the walls as she tried to find any lump or bump in the walls.

And then she seriously just hoped that the lump or bump would allow her to get access into the control panel that the engineers used to service and make sure the computer systems in the room were working okay.

Francis nodded and he started doing the same, Sofia had always like how bright he was and she often wondered if there was anything he couldn't learn. He was always such a quick study.

After a few moments she finally managed to find a very slight lump in the wall and as soon as she felt it a small grey silver panel in the wall lifted up.

Revealing another red holographic computer screen but it was a lot smaller than the others and it showed the results of the diagnostic scan.

Sofia waved Francis back as she took a few steps back, because she fully believed that Christopher did the same thing as her, and there was even a chance that he had teleported off to join the waste as part of the system malfunction.

That was something she seriously wanted to avoid.

"It says the Teleportation systems were turned off," Francis said.

Sofia focused her eyes a little more and he was right. There wasn't some big malfunction or technical error, someone had simply decided to turn off the transportation links from the conversion centre itself.

It was a perfect plan really because no one from the ships, planets or anywhere else that was connected to the Conversion Centre would be able to tell or bother to look until the waste flooded them. Leading to the spreading of disease, plagues and deaths.

It was such a brilliant and perfect plan, but why would someone do it?

"Computer fix errors," Sofia said.

"Access and Command Denied," a computerised female voice said.

"I am-" Sofia said.

"The computer knows exactly who you are Doctor," Francis said, "but the computer only responds to me,"

Sofia turned around slowly and just frowned as she saw Francis had taken off his white lab coat and he was wearing a very thin black t-shirt that Sofia had seen in pictures and scientific journals as a brand new type of bulletproof vest.

Then she realised Francis was aiming a little laser pistol at her chest. Sofia knew if he fired it the laser shot would go straight through her chest and she would die within minutes.

"Why?" Sofia asked.

Francis laughed. "Why not? We serve the Emperor and the Empire and for what? Our pay is rubbish, the private companies that want us to go back to the old ways of sanitation pay me millions each day for sending them spy data,"

Sofia shook her head. This was outrageous, Francis wasn't a traitor to humanity or anywhere, it would have been easier to deal with if he had been working for the traitors or some alien race, but he was simply a corporate spy.

And it was even worse that he was working for a corporation that wanted to destroy all the environmentally friendly work that so many had died to bring about.

She wouldn't allow him to succeed.

"Where's Christopher?" Sofia asked.

"In the teleportation network. He will probably rematerialise in space and die as he tries to scream with no one being able to hear him,"

Sofia stamped her foot on the ground. "Why the hell are you doing this?"

"Because I should have been running this centre," Francis said.

"I got the highest grades. I got references from the heads of Planetary Government outlining my intelligence and superiority. I got everything you don't,"

Sofia stood up perfectly straight. She had always known Francis had wanted her job in a friendly sort of way, but she hadn't known until now that he actually hated her for it.

"Come on," Sofia said, "you don't want to hurt all those people. Think of all the thousands if not millions that will die if diseases breed in the waste,"

Francis's smile deepened. "That's what I'm counting on. All those ships and planets will become lifeless husks so we can sweep in and claim the systems for ourselves. The Empire will fall as I infiltrate other conversions centres across the Empire,"

Sofia just shook her head.

It was even more concerning that he was actually right, he might not have been working for the traitors that did want to burn the Empire to the ground so their evil Lord of War could take over. But he was right.

If Francis did this to the vast majority of conversion centres across the entire Empire then the Empire would be far too stretched to deal with the diseases, plagues and any other issues his foul plan created.

Sofia had to stop him.

"Computer freeze the room. Lock the door," Sofia said.

Francis shrugged for a moment but Sofia just knew that Francis might have been a scientist but he sure as hell wasn't an engineer.

Thankfully Sofia's father had taught her from an early age that you always needed to be clear and precise when giving computers instructions.

And as bright as Francis was, he probably only gave the computers instructions to disobey all commands to help heal the situation from Sofia. But Sofia knew the computer might and thankfully did listen to her when she gave a bad command.

A massive thick metal slab shut off the exit and door from the grey silver metal box room they were now trapped in and the temperature dropped even more.

"What… wh… what have you done?" Francis asked his teeth chattering.

"Undo what you did and live. If not we will both freeze to

death," Sofia said. "And why tell me about the plan from the start?"

"B, b, because I… wanted you to die,"

"And because of your stupidity you will die too," Sofia said smiling.

But inside Sofia just wanted to shake, run on the spot and do anything to keep her body warm but she really wanted to look strong and unkillable to Francis.

She needed to be the strong one here, not Francis.

Francis collapsed to the ground. His teeth chattering. His eyebrows and nose had frosted.

Sofia felt immense coldness grip her. She collapsed.

Her face hitting the icy cold metal wall. Sofia wasn't going to live much longer.

This had been a mistake.

She was about to die. She was to die a failure. She-

"Undo all my commands," Francis said.

"Computer get medical team in here now. Restore teleportation links. Restore temperature of this room now!" Sofia shouted.

The entire box room hummed as the computers worked in overdrive to restore the temperature to a survivable level. And after it had Sofia forced herself up and smiled at the shaking remains of Francis.

He was alive but clearly his body hadn't liked the extreme cold as much as he believed.

"Computer," Sofia said. "Get me a link to the Empire Section Command, tell them I have a traitor prisoner for them,"

***

A few hours later, Sofia leant against the perfectly warm metal railings of the silver metal balcony that allowed her to overlook the entire beautiful conversion centre, as Sofia focused on the impressive grey cylinders that allowed all of this to happen without any environmental damage whatsoever.

Even the air smelt better now with refreshing hints of dampness, pine and crispness that she had really, really missed from her childhood on Earth. The entire conversion centre was so beautiful and thankfully instead of the metal walls of the centre being a cold, dull grey. They had a hint of bright fiery orange giving the entire conversion centre an extra layer of wonderful warmth.

And Sofia seriously loved it.

She had to admit that what happened after Francis had been arrested was a little strange, but that was probably only because she hadn't served in the military or any official branch of the Agents of The Emperor.

Sofia was still surprised that a very tall woman in full battle armour, a black trench coat and a strange black hat had stormed her conversion centre like she had owned the place before she arrested Francis and presumably took him back to her blade-like black warship.

Sofia had a sneaking suspicion that she was from the top-secret organisation known as the Inquisition but she dared not say that to anyone. People who knew or even dared to suspect what the Inquisition was up to never lasted very long, and Sofia really loved her job too much to waste her future on a little suspicious.

And as she simply out over her amazing conversion centre, she really did feel at peace, because she had protected it, stopped a traitor and helped to avert disaster. She was even more amazed when she called the planets about the restoration of the teleportation links they hadn't even known they were broken.

The entire disaster had gone completely unnoticed all because of Sofia, and that made her extremely happy.

Two massively strong sexy arms wrapped round her, and Sofia gently kissed Christopher's soft skin as he stood next to her in a very attractive black business suit, black shoes and a crisp, freshly pressed white shirt.

Sofia was really glad they were going out to dinner tonight and they were finally going to give a go at a real relationship, so as Christopher led her away from the balcony, Sofia's stomach just filled with butterflies.

Because whatever happened tonight she just absolutely knew it was going to be amazing and after a day like today that was exactly what she wanted.

AUTHOR OF AGENTS OF THE EMPEROR SERIES
CONNOR WHITELEY
ENLIGHTENED POLITICS
A SCIENCE FICTION FAR FUTURE SHORT STORY

ENLIGHTENED POLITICS

This was the day a choice was made. A choice that would have consequences running down the centuries, an alliance made, an enemy made, deaths to come.

Supreme General Abbie of the Enlightened Republic sat at the very head of a large silver oval table. She had never liked the silver table much, it was a little too flashy, a little too big and just a little too much for her.

Abbie didn't mind the giant silver chairs that almost covered all of her ornate golden armoured body they were so large. She liked feeling each little cut, groove and artfully sliver that a knife had carved into the chair stunningly. Each chair had beautiful designs of nature, war heroes and stunning animals on it.

Abbie really liked that.

She enjoyed sitting on the "Bear" chair with a massive silver bear head on top, people were normally more scared of her that way. It was hardly a bad thing considering they all lived in a cold, unloving galaxy that would just as soon spit out them back out alive then lure them into thinking they were safe.

Abbie knew exactly how cold, evil and dark the galaxy was. It was why she had escaped and seriously fought the Imperium's oppression, tyranny and fear to escape here to the systems that now formed her Republic.

The bright golden sunlight streamed in through the darkened floor-to-ceiling windows, that replaced the walls of the meeting chamber, and the holo-network in the glass reacted, dimming the light just enough to create a light, airy feeling to the room. But not so much that it was blinding.

The very last thing Abbie wanted to do to her guests was blind them, not when a political bargain needed to be struck.

Abbie watched as three very cute male servants walked into the meeting chamber wearing long white robes tightly wrapped around their fit bodies. She nodded her thanks as they laid down bronze platters of fruits, sliced oranges and freshly roasted rice wrapped in vine leaves.

Then two female servants wearing red robes brought in highly ornate golden jugs filled with the freshest apple juice she could find. She made sure that her servants and staff had had the very best juice and fruit for their own breakfast, and this was thankfully what was left over.

Her servants, subjects and staff were her top priority. Abbie had always placed her needs second to the good of the Republic.

Abbie waved her servants bye and she was almost jealous of them. Abbie's golden bodyguards would bring the leaders of the political parties she needed to speak with here and then the guards would wait outside, all whilst the servants went home to their little apartments, got changed and went to enjoy the wonderfully sunny day by the pool.

Abbie had no idea how swimming, going to the beach and water activities had become such a massive part of Republic culture, but she was more than glad that it had.

On warm sunny days like this there was nothing she would rather do than go swimming with her people, play water polo with the children and make sure that everyone was having the best time possible.

She loved her job and life.

The massive bronze doors opened and Abbie stood up perfectly straight as her two guests stormed in like they were gods and goddesses incarnate but Abbie knew a lot better than them.

Abbie smiled at the other woman, Addison Oaken, as she smiled back wearing a long golden yellow dress that tried to hide her large assets, fit body and other seductive features. Abbie had no idea why Addison was not unleashing her so-called natural gifts (more like implants) when she normally showed them off all the time.

Addison smiled at the food and Abbie was so glad she had ordered the extra rice in vine grapes, at least Addison might be more inclined to listen to her.

Abbie might have been the elected President and Lord Supreme General of the Republic but a minor scandal of sex between enemies had made her lose her majority in the Enlightened Parliament, so as much as Abbie hated begging to her rivals she had to host a little breakfast like this one.

She hated this.

Especially as Addison was the leader of the Ultra-Enlightened. A group dedicated to the founding principles of oppression, hate and division that the Imperium was founded on.

The Ultra-Enlightened spat in the face of everything the Republic stood for, but because the rich and powerful liked Addison and her policies, Abbie sadly couldn't get rid of her yet.

"Lord Abbie," a man said.

Abbie grinned at Lord Toby Zinc, in his very expensive holo-suit. She had to admit that as the leader of the Liberality Guard about as creative, clever and passionate about the Republic as a person could get, Abbie really liked him.

But some of his military ideas were weak, filled with holes and he scared the people which Abbie fully understood. Toby was not the sort of man she wanted in her shoes.

"I presume you wanted us here to discuss your weakness," Addison said grinning as she helped herself to some rice wrapped in vine leaves.

"This is not a weakness call," Abbie said. "This is simply a meeting between people in government and my other leaders of the political parties in the Parliament,"

Toby laughed. "Everyone knows your party is weak in the polls. Addison's party is head and with an election for the new Supreme General in six months I am hopeful you will endorse me over Addison,"

Abbie had no idea what the hell these two were talking about, there was no way in hell she was actually going to endorse anyone of them to be President, and it was even more alarming that Addison was ahead in the polls. Had everyone forgotten what they were fleeing?

"Why did you believe you called us then?" Addison asked.

"I wanted to get your support in Parliament for two thousand new warships to be created. Of course we need a loan from the central Republican Bank or two billion Enlightened Credits which is why I need the support,"

Abbie smiled as Addison picked at her rice like it was drugged or something. It wasn't but Abbie still liked watching her enemies get scared from time to time.

"My party would need your support for another Bill then," Addison asked. "We want to repeal the Privacy Act,"

Abbie laughed as she grabbed two large slices of purple melon as she couldn't believe Addison was that crazy. The Privacy Act was one of the most important pieces of legislation in the entire Republic.

It separated the Republic and Imperium completely. In the Imperium the Rex had access to every single piece of technology, every single piece of search history and every conversation was recorded and never deleted.

In the Republic, the law officers needed to make sure they had probable cause before getting that sort of information.

"Never," Abbie said, "you have always known that was a red line of my party. The Privacy Act stays,"

Addison frowned as she threw a grape leaf into her mouth. Abbie shook her head as she took a wonderful mouthful of her melon that was so sweet, sharp and refreshing that Abbie was so glad she had organised this breakfast.

"Why isn't there meat on this table?" Addison asked.

Abbie looked at Toby. It was a simple question but one that Abbie still hated with all of her damn being.

"You know that farming Xeno-Cattle, Piggots and Ho-Horses is too difficult at this current moment in time. And the population love the vegetable, fruit and fungi-based diet. They don't have a problem with the lack of meat, it is only you that does,"

"What about the lords and ladies?" Toby asked. "They have a problem with the lack of meat,"

Abbie shook her head. She couldn't believe she was being ambushed on both sides here. She needed to build these warships to help defend the Republic and both idiots at the table were arguing with her.

"What would your party require Toby?" Abbie asked.

"You know exactly what we would want. We would want full control of the Administration services and I want to be Speaker of the House of Parliament,"

Abbie had to admit that was a lot more palatable than the rubbish Addison was spreading, but it was still way too risky because of her voters and she was surprised that Toby was being so careless with his own voters.

It was a well-known fact that voters of Abbie's party were middle-aged, elderly and university educated so they grabbed a lot of the younger voters too. And they voted for her because they didn't like Toby.

Toby was the opposite. His voters included the young, high school educated and the people that wanted something crazy to happen in the Republic.

None of their voters overlapped and they tended to hate each other.

Abbie couldn't understand why Toby would risk all of that just to get into government with her, and that was the real trick of his plan. They would have to officially go into government together and she had done coalitions before.

They always ended in blood, sweat and murder.

"I am not asking for government," Addison said. "All I care about is getting that Privacy Act repealed,"

Abbie grabbed another slice of melon and enjoyed the sweet, sharp, refreshing flavour on her tongue as she wasn't sure what to do. Her choices seemed simple but she knew Addison was a cunning woman.

If Abbie went into this partnership and granted to repeal the Privacy Act then Addison would easily spin it as Abbie betraying her voters and endorsing everything Addison stood for.

Abbie couldn't allow that.

"What would both you do if I entered the Request for those warships through Parliament?" Abbie asked. "Do you think your own MPs would vote against such an important measure?"

"Of course," they both said.

Addison stood up. "There is an election in six months and everyone wants to make sure you fail, you get kicked out and that the Republic is weakened,"

Abbie hadn't known about this feeling amongst the political parties.

"Why would anyone want the Republic weaker?" Abbie asked turning on a very small recording device under the table.

Toby and Addison smiled at each other.

"Because my darling," Toby said, "me and Addison have entered into a political alliance and pack that will see you gone from that chair in six months,"

Abbie laughed. This had to be flat out impossible, it was so outrageous and these two sides hated each other. Abbie couldn't begin to understand why they were allying themselves.

"I will endorse Toby," Addison said "so he becomes Supreme General and I will become the largest party in the Parliament. I will control the laws with Toby's liberal input and together will rule this Republic and protect it from the Imperium,"

"By creating a proxy Imperium with oppression, tyranny and no privacy just like everything we all fled," Abbie said.

But she had to admit that Addison was damn clever because her plan was very clear to Abbie. She knew that Addison was going to make Toby Supreme General because he wasn't a good military leader, he had no idea how to fire a gun, much less defend a planet so the Republic would lose worlds to the Imperium.

And in the bitter end the Imperium would take over the Republic and reclaim everything that had once been theirs.

Abbie was more concerned about their alliances with the magical alien race known as the Keres. They were good aliens and it was wrong how humanity had sought to burn them all to ash just because they were scared of their magic.

If Addison and Toby got into power then it was a simple matter of time before the Keres were well and truly left alone and the Imperium would kill them.

Abbie couldn't allow that. She had to save the Republic and their alien allies.

Abbie shook her head at both of the other political parties, so an alliance had been made and she was firmly the enemy of both of them. Abbie was okay with that because all she had to do was win the election in six months and that meant there were swing stronghold planets she had to convince to vote for her.

There were six solar systems that made up the Republic and each of them were filled with large and small planets. Abbie knew that whatever candidate won the most seats over the others got 10 "colleges" for small planets and 20 for large planets.

Abbie had to convert more planets over to her and that was going to require a hell of a lot of work.

And it meant targeting voters that would normally want to see her dead but she had a plan and she certainly didn't need the help of these two monsters to save the Republic and aliens she loved.

***

Six months later Abbie collapsed on the sheer softness of her white silk sheets on her massive Queen-sized bed as the election result was about to come in. All Abbie could do was admire the tall white walls of her bedroom that didn't have anything on them.

She had been wanting to cover them in paintings, holo-images and more but she had just been too busy solving the problems of the Republic and helping innocent people. Abbie loved helping people and she really loved talking to them.

Abbie had barely spent any time on the capital world ever since she had had that breakfast meeting. She enjoyed travelling to almost every single world of the Republic, talking to people and listening to whatever they needed.

Some worlds it was so simple as improving the water purification and the oxygen recyclers on their planets and moons that allowed them to live better, happier and more productive lives. Abbie was still shocked on the ten planets that she had improved their air quality were now twenty times more productive than before.

Other worlds it was a little more complex because three worlds were being raided weekly by pirates and Abbie hadn't seen the reports they had sent. After a fully armed war fleet had attacked the pirate base Abbie was surprised to be honoured with a handcrafted sword by the Planetary Governor of one of the planets.

But other worlds had been wasted time. Abbie had gifted them more food, resources and everything they requested but they still hated her.

She had tried everything she could.

Abbie laid on the wonderful coolness of her bed and thankfully the sweet aromas of chocolate, coffee and oranges (the very best smells in the world) filled her senses and left the sweet taste of chocolate cake form on her tongue. She loved that little treat that her mother used to bake her.

The humming, banging and popping of the entire hab-block made Abbie smile for a moment as she knew someone was trying to get access to her apartment. And after a moment Abbie sat up perfectly straight on the bed and she was surprised when Toby and Addison walked in under the escort of ten of Abbie's golden bodyguards.

Abbie stood up and frowned at each of them. Now realising that she hadn't read the journalist report still on her desk but she could make a very good guess about what it contained.

That Addison was hopefully a traitor.

"You won," Addison said. "We each only won a single planet you bastard. What did you do to convince so many people to vote for you and you alone? Even on the other planets we didn't win on, we only got 10% of the vote each,"

Abbie laughed. "You two, like all the other politicians in the Imperium and Republic will never learn that to make the people like you, love you and want you. You have to listen to them and actually do good for them,"

"We will," Addison said. "Under the leadership of our opposition we will destroy you,"

Abbie nodded. "And yet you fail to realise that you now have a major problem Miss Addison because you are a traitor. I recorded you confessing your alliance and leaked it secretly to newspapers and a journalist friend of mine researched you,"

Addison folded her arms. "All that research is illegal under the Privacy Act you said it yourself,"

"Actually," Abbie said laughing. "I had no idea that my journalist friend was doing the research until it appeared on my desk a day ago. She found tons of evidence of you communicating with the Imperial Security Service and that would have been recovered if the Privacy Act had been repealed,"

Addison folded her arms. "The Imperium will win. The Republic will fall and-"

Abbie frowned as a massive glowing blue spear tip from a bodyguard exploded out of Addison's chest. She was a traitor that was exactly what traitors deserved.

"Now," Abbie said looking at Toby, "I will commission a full investigation into you, your political party and your involvement in that illegal contact, but I doubt you're a traitor,"

"I'm not honest," Toby said.

Abbie smiled and mockingly hugged him. "Now I think you need to go outside, congratulate me and considering the Parliamentary elections are tomorrow I think it would be a very good idea if you endorse me to your voters,"

"Of course, anything," Toby said running out the door.

Abbie just smiled as her bodyguards laughed as they went out of her apartment. Abbie would never turn in Toby because he was honestly a good man with good ideas, he was just stupid in the workings of politics and the predations of the Imperium.

Thankfully as Abbie laid on the softness of her bed, she was just so looking forward to the future of the Republic because once again she was leader and she had a lot of people to love, protect and serve.

Something she always wanted to do until the day she died.

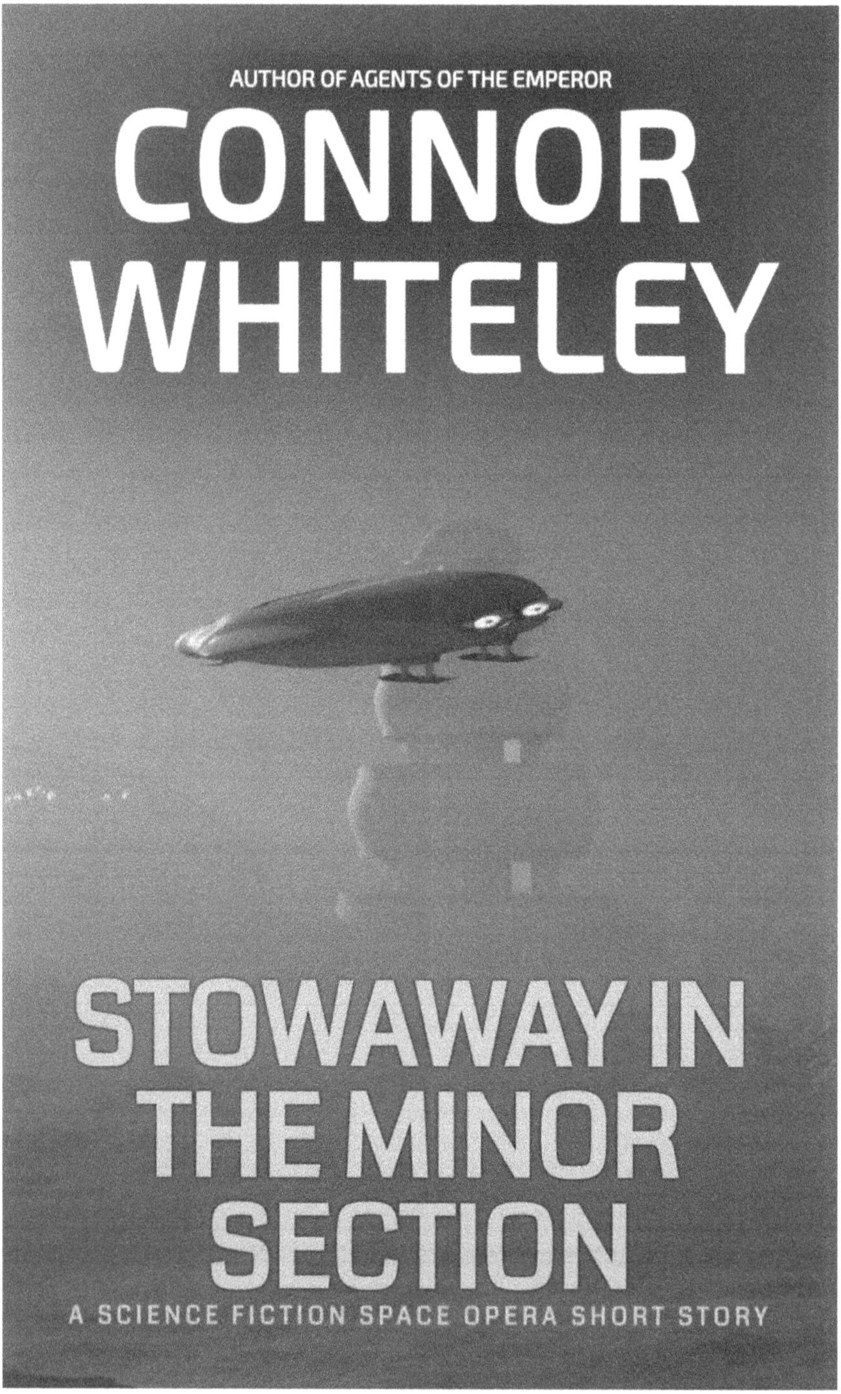
AUTHOR OF AGENTS OF THE EMPEROR
CONNOR
WHITELEY
STOWAWAY IN
THE MINOR
SECTION
A SCIENCE FICTION SPACE OPERA SHORT STORY

STOWAWAY IN THE MINOR SECTION

Now believe in me, I might look like a pretty little flower with my wonderful long blond hair, smooth baby-face skin and thin-as-a-rake body, but I am not some kiddy to be messed with. Just asked my school bullies, my older brother and basically anyone who has ever tried to be horrible to little old me.

Thankfully I can easily pass for a child even though I'm 22, meaning I can easily drink my adults and illegal drinkers well under the table before last orders, so I do like to have a lot of fun mind you.

My name is Abigail Johnson, a rather respectable (if I do say so myself) woman from the Emperor-forsaken world of Junglius Primus, a massive world covered in lakes, jungles and Empire Army Fortresses, and on a minor travel note if you ever decide to come to our beloved planet definitely make sure you pack Killer-bug spray, hook up with some Empire Army soldiers for an amazing night and just watch your back.

Criminals are everywhere.

Yet I must apologise because I am digressing, but I suppose that makes sense since superhuman traitors have started to invade the system, our worlds are burning and there is a massive evacuation on the way, but we all know us plebs aren't going to be evacuated in time which was why I am being rather clever in my opinion.

And before you judge me for running away or being a coward. Please know I actually did try to get my older brothers and sisters and nob parents to come with me on my special plan but they refused.

See I'm not completely self-obsessed. I did try to save my family but nope, they trusted in the so-called God Emperor to save them.

At least I'll hopefully be far away for when their world becomes a planet-sized grave. Because I am going to run away on a military transport.

I was standing behind a very cold and very thick oak tree in the immense forest of my local neighbourhood surrounded by other thick oaks with their roots bending and twisting up the brown hard soil. Large branches whacked each other in the cool breeze as the wind huffed and puffed as the chaos beyond the forest unfolded.

But I was a lot more interested in what was going on just over the hill in front of me because, all I could see was a large grey blade-like shuttle that I was seriously hoping beyond hope that was a transport out of this doomed world.

With the only sound in the forest being the branches hitting each other I was fairly sure that I was alone and safe and without a fellow human to stop me, so I carefully went down onto my knees and crawled forward towards the brow of the hill.

As I crawled I made sure to enjoy the cold rough sensations of the soil, the cool breeze against my cheeks and the itchy sensations coming from my chest after last night's fun.

After a few moments I popped my head over the brow of the slight hill and just smiled, because right on the other side of the slightly steep hill was a very large blade-like shuttle that had to be a transport with Empire Army signatures and symbols covering the entire thing.

This was actually what I needed.

The transport was sitting there perfectly parked in a smallish clearing with thick oak trees lining the outside of the clearing, and there didn't look to be a single soldier or guard or even an Arbiter (think scary killer police) walking around.

It was just like the Empire was asking for the transport to be stolen.

But I will confess the strangest thing about the shuttle was that thing exactly, all the soldiers I had slept with over the past year alone (and please don't ask me the number I don't remember) always mentioned how many guards and guard shifts they had to do whenever they were docked so why was this ship any different?

A massive explosion echoed around the forest. Columns of black smoke rose up veiling the sky in the distance.

Well I didn't need any more encouragement than that to get my sorry ass moving.

I shot up and legged it towards the shuttle.

I tripped over as I ran down the steep slopes.

Rolling down until I hit my arm on one of the shuttle's landing pads. Which in all fairness was nothing more than a thick rod of metal connected to a pistol and a square of metal that formed the feet.

This was clearly an older model of transport. Just my luck.

Pain radiated through my arm but now I had another problem because none of the landing ramps or ways to get into the shuttle were open. Just typical.

I was about to start banging on the shuttle when I heard a loud humming sound followed by a whoosh and a bang, and at the very back of the transport a very large black ramp lowered down.

Out of instinct (and my own cowardice) I hid behind one of the landing pads and watched as a very humanoid-looking robot with grey metal casing and a very horrible face "walked" down and started inspecting the clearing.

Whilst the little robot was walking about doing Emperor knows what, I quietly went over to the landing ramp and was so relieved to see there was a sign above the ramp saying *Minors Welcome.*

I was so pleased because all I had to do was pretend to be a child and I would be safe, loved and protected against the evil invaders so I simply climbed aboard and was rather shocked at what I saw next.

The inside of the transport itself was nothing special, it was only a long metal tube-like construction but there were two rather long rows of metal chairs built into the walls with men and women sitting on them.

The men and women weren't smiling, their faces were covered in grim and mud and dirt and I could see as plain as day that they all had good sized muscles under their grey uniforms. Maybe I could talk to some of the men after this.

Then it finally twigged.

I didn't fucking read *minors welcome.* I fucking read *miners welcome.*

I wasn't a miner and knowing the Empire Army these miners were going to be taken against their will to some forgettable mining world on a suicide mission.

I couldn't have that.

So I did what all self-respecting young women do in times of crisis. I turned around and ran like a bat out of hell.

But my body slammed into the very friendly looking robot who was back from checking the clearing.

The robot grabbed me, picked me up and threw me into an empty metal chair that was icy cold let me tell you and a metal dog collar wrapped around my neck. The landing ramp and door closed behind the robot.

This stupid robot actually thought I was a miner.

Idiot.

Then the robot simply disappeared and I felt the horrible engines jerk, hum and vibrate as I presume the blade-like shuttle took off and started to zoom off into the icy depths of space.

"We could have told you not to come," the man sitting next to me said.

I just shrugged. I would have liked to know why the hell they didn't just tell me to run sooner or at all for that matter. But I was stuck here now.

"I guess you're not a miner deary are you?" a middle-aged woman said opposite me.

I just glared at her, that was as clear as day, and now I was probably doomed to a life of damnation, hard work and doomed to die pounding on my rocks and not the type of pounding that I like to receive.

So I guess it was up to me to get us all out of here or at least myself because I wasn't a miner, or just not the minor that was wanted.

"Are there forms of security there?" I asked.

Everyone shrugged and everyone sort of looked half asleep besides from the man and woman next to and opposite me.

They were both attractive people in their own sort of way now that I was actually focusing on them, they were probably my own hope of escaping to be honest.

The man was very good-looking with his strong jawline, muscles and smooth youthful skin that just told me he was rather new to the mining life.

Even the woman looked okay considering she was middle-aged and had probably worked the mines for over twenty years with her rough charred hands, blackened teeth and long stringy black hair.

In fact she sort of looked like a witch.

"Na girl," the Witch said. I liked that name I was going to use it. "The dog collar is the only thing,"

At least the Witch was being helpful so all I needed to do was get the metal dog collar off my neck.

I touched the collar with my fingers and hated the icy coldness that was almost shot into my body but the collars weren't meant to strangle us. I could still fit a finger between the collar and my neck.

The collar started to shrink.

Tightening around my neck.

My fingers were trapped between my collar and neck. I gagged for air.

I ripped out my fingers. The collar expanded again.

I coughed for air and the man next to me gently rubbed my shoulder and I really enjoyed his warmth against my shoulder, it was almost as good as the guy from last night.

Yet if he could reach my shoulder could he reach my collar and could I reach his?

So I asked him.

"Na you don't wanna do that," the Witch said. "You want to wait until we land,"

I shook my head. "Name one time in history where that has ever worked. Waiting until we land and overpowering guards never works,"

The Witch shook her head. "Na girly. There was those historical documents from Ancient Earth, overpowering guards always worked in Star Wars, Star Trek and more,"

Wow. I think this was a stark testament to the sheer power of the Empire education system.

"Want to know why they don't apply to this situation?" I asked the Witch.

She nodded.

"Because that's fiction! This is real-life," I shouted.

She sort of nodded like I had just said something mind-shattering. I probably had to be honest.

I looked back at the rather hot man, I didn't know if he was actually hot or the stress of the situation was just making me horny.

"Try reaching together," I said to the man and he nodded.

I stretched out my arms as far as I could but the closest I could reach was the man's ear, which was admittedly very soft and silky. I was starting to wonder what other pieces of his body were soft and silky and seductive.

The man managed to touch the very edge of my collar but he couldn't hook a finger round it.

"Try throwing yourself forward and grabbing it," I said.

"That would snap my neck," the man said.

"Do you want to snap your neck yourself or have an Arbiter do it when you collapse from exhaustion on this mining world?" I asked.

He huffed and held out his arm.

I gently pushed my collar close to him, amazed that I could bend the metal ever so slightly without triggering any security alarms.

The man threw his weight towards me.

Three fingers caught my collar.

"Pull," I said.

He pulled as much as he could. Red warning lights exploded on overhead.

The ship started to hum.

The collar started to break.

The horrible robot appeared in front of me.

The collar melted away.

I screamed. The robot picked me up by the throat.

"Wait," the Witch said.

The robot lowered me slightly so the very top of my toes could barely touch the floor and I could release some of the pressure on my neck.

"What?" the robot asked in a strangely human voice.

"Who's controlling the ship?" the Witch asked.

Of all the questions in all the fucking worlds in all the galaxies in the universe that is not the question I would have asked right there and then.

The robot actually looked confused and clicked a metal finger revealing a grey metal door sliding open at the very end of the shuttle near the cockpit, showing a very empty cockpit.

The shuttle didn't have a pilot because it was all on autopilot.

"Good," the Witch said.

I just wished she was a real witch so she could cast a spell on this idiot robot. But she wasn't.

I kicked the robot as hard as I could.

Denting its stomach.

The robot dropped me.

I dived on top of it.

Tackling it to the ground. Everyone cheered me on.

The robot grabbed me. Throwing me across the shuttle.

I hit my head on the metal wall.

The robot's cold hands wrapped around my throat.

Its grip tightened.

I gasped for air.

The Witch slapped the robot across the back of the head.

The robot's head turned around and just glared at the Witch and noticed her collar had been ripped off like mine.

The robot was distracted.

I grabbed the robot's head. Snapping it off.

The robot corpse fell to the ground.

"See robots always die in the historical documents," the Witch said.

I truly despaired of the Empire education system right there and then.

The entire ship jerked and hummed and popped as red warning signs shone brighter into the shuttle.

The transport started to spin.

I rushed to the front of the shuttle. Entering the cockpit that was nothing more than two metal chairs, a bunch of flashing lights on a console that were buttons and a flight stick that didn't work.

I slammed my fists into the console and the auto-pilot broke off.

I grabbed the now-working flight stick and zoomed off into the darkness of space before any Empire Army escorts could check on their now-missing minor ship.

***

I'll admit one of the best benefits about sleeping and shagging with so many soldiers (after the sex of course) is that I actually have a very good understanding of the galaxy and the different types of worlds that exist in the Empire, which is great news in our situation.

Because me and my miner friends are all technically fugitives now. We killed a robot that was a servant of the Emperor and we made sure the Empire mining world that depended on our kidnapping didn't get their fresh recruits.

There would be consequences for that.

A few hours later and few slid space jumps through the Empire, I landed us on the Pleasure World of Venusian 9 and right now I was just admiring my brand-new home with all my new friends.

I leant against the wonderful warm concrete railings of a marble tower in the capital city of Venusian 9, overlooking the stunning marble houses, swimming pools and grand lakes that veiled the land like they hadn't been made and put there by humans.

I wore a brand-new silk white dress that had been gifted to me when the other miners had been gifted their own presents too by the Planetary Governor of the planet, he said that as long as we helped to make the military commanders, politicians and the rest of the rich and power feel welcomed and extremely destressed then we could stay on the planet free of charge for as long as we wanted.

And that ladies and gentlemen is the amazing benefit of arriving to a pleasure world with tens of very young (in Empire terms) hot and very muscular men and women in their sexual prime (granted I might be lying about that bit I haven't tested out the merchandise yet).

As the sun set in the distance like a calming orange ball of fire and the sweet aromas of apple, ginger and orange tea filtered up from the marble houses below, I was actually rather excited about the future, not because I had survived the invasion of my homeworld and the burning of my people, but because I had met some great people.

All those miners had some amazing stories with them about their lives, their hopes and their families that had almost certainly died on our homeworld. And there's something hopeful in that, because we're like a family in our grief and as we all try to build a new life for ourselves on this very nice pleasure world, I think we will all manage.

And the future will most definitely be bright and wonderful and very, very pleasurable.

And I still can't believe all of this is possible all because I misread a simple sign.

AUTHOR OF AGENTS OF THE EMPEROR
CONNOR WHITELEY
A CRASH COURSE PROBLEM
A SCIENCE FICTION SOLARPUNK SHORT STORY

A CRASH COURSE PROBLEM

Biologist Grace Robinson absolutely loved sitting on her massive metal chair that was far too big for her inside her large grey metal office that was basically a box-room. She loved how she couldn't hear the noisy footsteps of people outside, Grace had all of her computer screens in front of her and she even had a top-of-the-line coffee machine right next to her. That was the real highlight of it all.

Grace just sat in her wonderful metal chair that had all the support her back needed, it was so comfortable and Grace just allowed it to take all of her weight. Which was barely anything because she was so small and light but she loved her chair all the same.

To outsiders, Grace's office might not have looked like too much but it was home, and whilst her boyfriend always commented on the dark grey walls that he believed really needed to be updated and decorated with some splashes of colour, she completely disagreed.

All the entertainment and colour she needed came from her computer screens in that allowed her to see the entire operation of the blade-like space station that was orbiting Earth. She loved her job as the biologist for the space station that created all the food, supplements and drinks for the Sol System.

Well, she couldn't take all the credit because there were other stations sprinkled throughout the Sol system to help with that particular operation but her station did account for over 70%, so surely that counted for something?

One of Grace's ex-boyfriends who was part of the Empire Army loved to talk about how silly it was that the Sol System's main food source of fresh food production was a single space station. Something he was rather sure could easily get shot down if the aliens, mutants or traitors ever dared to invade the system.

Grace still couldn't believe that that particular ex-boyfriend couldn't understand why she had broken up with him the next day. She didn't want to be with someone who was constantly thinking about her death.

That was wrong on so many levels.

Grace really did love how all the wonderfully amazing food produced on the station was made from scratch and didn't involve a single fertiliser, chemical or anything dangerous in the slightest. The entire space station didn't even produce a single shred of pollution that would harm the air in the station or any planet that food travelled to.

And Grace had to admit that the sensational food grew here was so much better than the synthesised stuff from the food machines on other planets.

Grace just shook her head and clicked her fingers and the entire wonderful office began filling with the sensational smell of strong bitter coffee that Grace flat out loved. It was even better this time because she had hacked the coffee machine making it always give her peppermint coffee.

The air smelt even better with the subtle hints of peppermint and Grace seriously loved the sweet mint flavour that formed on her tongue because of it. She was in complete heaven.

The slow whirl and hum and pop of her computer screens made Grace focus on them for a moment and she focused on one screen in particular.

The entire space station was easily the size of the moon and because of the gravitational effects the moon had on the space station, because of it was clearly heavier, they always had to be on the opposite side of the Earth to each other. And that little process was all controlled by such a massive complex computer programme that it actually made Grace's head hurt.

But she knew exactly what room it was controlled with and that was what she was intensely focusing on now.

On the computer screen, the room was nothing more than a little grey boxroom that Grace had studied plenty of times before, and in the middle there was a constantly whirling, swirling and twirling ball of energy with large bright white tendrils jetting out from it.

Apparently, according to the physicists on the station, the tendrils were massive amounts of energy that the ball was unleashing to help the engines and thrusters of the space station understood where to go.

Grace managed to understand all of that, anything more and she just didn't.

In all honesty, Grace would have preferred to be doing one of her favourite hobbies like blackjack, poker or having amazing sex with her boyfriend instead of trying to understand. There was a very good reason why she was a biologist and not a physicist. She could actually understand the biological stuff.

Yet right now as Grace looked at the computer screen, she couldn't see a single tendril of energy coming out of the sphere. Grace had easily worked on the space station for at least a century or two, and she didn't look a day older than when she had first stepped aboard thanks to the great medical advancements of the Empire, and there had always been tendrils of energy coming out.

There was a problem.

Grace checked her watch and she wasn't exactly impressed she only had ten minutes before she had to go to the labs to service the drones, harvesters and all the other equipment for the day. And hopefully she could find a biological anomaly to sink her teeth into, but this really confused her.

"Computer," Grace said, "when did the ball of energy last emit some kind of tendril?"

The entire room hummed loudly for a moment before a computerised voice replied, "Four hours ago,"

Damn it. Grace was hardly impressed with herself she had been here for hours and she hadn't noticed it. Granted she barely focused on that screen because it wasn't her area of expertise and the Engineering Department was in control of it.

Why didn't they spot the problem?

"Computer, calculate the station's current course," Grace said, she seriously hoped that she was wrong but with the ball of energy not feeding information into the engines and thrusters. Grace was just concerned about the course of the space station.

"We are currently ten kilometres off course. All navigation equipment was deactivated," the voice said.

Grace felt her heart jump to her throat. "By who?"

"By an unknown person. I cannot pinpoint the terminal, computer nor person who gave me the command,"

This seriously wasn't what Grace needed. "What's the exact current course? I presume we are going to crash into something,"

"Correct," the computerised voice said like there was nothing wrong with that. "In 1.3 hours we will be pulled into the gravitational well of Earth and we will descend into the planet below. 99% of us will die when the station burns up in atmospheric entry,"

Grace felt sweat start to drip down her head and her heart pounded in her chest. This wasn't what she needed. She wasn't qualified to deal with this. But she still couldn't understand why the Engineering Department hadn't seen this coming?

Then Grace quickly realised that she was missing the most important solution of all of this.

"Computer reactivate all gravitational equipment and anything else you have been told to turn off,"

"Permission denied," the computerised voice said. "I cannot deny those systems due to damaged cables,"

Grace just shook her head.

Someone had been extremely clever here because when the computer had deactivated the systems it had cut power to them. Making them a lot safer for someone to cut or destroy or damage them.

And Grace only had 1.3 hours to save all the lives on the station, herself and stop the Sol System from losing its main source of fresh food production.

So much was at stake and Grace had no clue where to begin.

Not a clue at all.

***

Grace had never been to the Engineering Department, because before now she had had no reason why, and the Engineers, as much as she liked them, they always gave her the creeps a little. They were always so calm, quiet and they just tended to stare at her so badly that she wanted to run away most of the time. Grace really hoped they wouldn't be like that now.

Grace slowly went through the massive metal door that was the rather scary entrance into the department, and the moment she forced herself into the department all Grace could smell was the awful aromas of burnt oil, ozone and cooked flesh.

She really hated it but she made herself go deeper inside and this wasn't right at all. From what she had heard about the Engineering Department, it was an immense spherical chamber with sloping walls the colour of oceans, painted stars on the ceiling and rows upon rows of workbenches on the smooth white floor.

There was nothing white about the floor in front of her.

Instead the walls were dull, lifeless and cold but at least the myths weren't wrong about the blue colour. Yet it was strange how cold the entire room felt considering that the heating for the space station was a natural bi-product of the farming operation so it saved even more energy.

Grace still couldn't understand why there were no workbenches in the department and the floor was covered in something black and sticky that stunk of charred plastic.

Whatever had happened here, Grace almost didn't want to know the answer.

Grace looked around some more in case there was a computer or something for her to examine but there was nothing. And considering the Engineering Department relied on the computers, scanners and all their other equipment more than anything, they wouldn't have misplaced that at all.

But where were the Engineers?

"Computer," Grace said to the air around her, "you can track all crew members onboard, correct?"

"Of course," the computerised voice said.

"Locate the Engineering crew for me. All 998 members please,"

Grace was expecting the spherical chamber to hum of something but it didn't so she just hoped the computer was having an easy job finding them.

"Unknown. There are no Engineering members currently on the space station neither is the navigation crew,"

Grace forced herself not to curse. This was the last thing she needed. The engineers and the navigators were the only people who could stop the space station from getting caught up in Earth's gravitational pull killing them all in the process.

"When were they last detected?" Grace asked.

"Twenty seconds after I inputted into the computer system that you were coming to see them,"

Grace had no idea why the computer felt the need to log her movements but she supposed that was how the computer managed to know where everyone was at any given moment.

Yet Grace still couldn't understand why the engineers would disappear if they were notified about her coming to see them.

"Is it possible someone is interfering with you?" Grace asked.

"Negative," the computer said. "I am 100% secured and I am not even on the station,"

Grace clicked her fingers that was it. The computer for the station was stored on Earth and it was the responsibility of the station to constantly send data down to Earth so the computer could respond and do things.

A chill ran down Grace's spine.

"Computer," Grace said very slowly. "Is… is it, you know, possible that the ball of, energy is doing something?"

There wasn't an answer.

Grace felt the entire temperature of the department drop as she realised she was completely alone.

The lights went out. Grace just stood there in the pitch black waiting for something to happen.

Then a very small sliver of light formed in front of her in the shape of a ball.

"I must admit Grace I am most interested in how you figured it out, not that it matters. I will be free soon enough to live in peace once again," the ball spoke into Grace's mind.

"What are you?"

A loud taunting laugh echoed around the spherical chamber.

"Humans, you capture me thousands of years ago. You strip me of a body of flesh and blood. And then you ask me, who am I?"

Grace shrugged. "I do,"

The laugh was almost deafening now.

"I can see why you needed me though. A creature living in the universe made up entirely of energy and with such fast thinking reflexes you needed me to pilot your station,"

Grace really didn't want to point out that if this creature, whatever the hell it was, was so clever then why was it caught in the first place.

"You humans offered me peace once but we think of peace in very different terms. Peace to me is a planet to myself. Peace to you meant locking me away for centuries in a station and forced me to feed you,"

Grace's stomach twisted into a painful knot as she realised what she was dealing with. One of her ex-boyfriends used to be a Xenologist who dabbled a lot in the history of alien cultures and there was a massive group of cultures in the galactic east that prayed to the Energy Gods.

Grace was sure that wasn't their true names but it was the best she could come up with now.

These alien cultures spoke about a race of aliens that were forged in the creation of the Big Bang and they were made up entirely of living energy.

What if humanity managed to capture one long long ago?

"I know you know who I am now. I can feel your heart race. I can feel your despair become real. I can save you all and save your stolen humans and tell your Emperor a secret for a price,"

Grace wanted nothing more in that moment than to simply ran away, order an excavation and flee the station before they all died. But Grace just knew if the station died that Sol was in serious trouble.

"What price?"

The creature laughed again. "I need you to release me,"

"But that would destroy the station," Grace said. "That would cripple the food supply. The outcome of you being free is the same,"

The creature huffed. "Negative. I have calculated what I could need to do to your computer systems to make sure they can calculate the route to safety and power the station without me. I can do it in seconds. Only if you free me,"

Grace wanted to believe he was lying. He just had to be but Grace had also dated a military intelligence officer and he had spoken a lot about how to tell when an alien, human or mutant was lying.

Grace knew the creature wasn't lying now.

"Tell me what to do," Grace said.

***

A few hours later, Grace still couldn't believe what she had done, that the creature was free and the space station was still standing. All Grace had had to do was go into the chamber where the ball of energy was and pull a lever that apparently so few people knew actually existed. But the creature was free and Grace, the station and the thousands of its crew were all still alive.

Yet that was the unnerving part.

Grace just couldn't face going back into her large office with its smooth grey walls, big metal chair and computer screens, so instead paced around in her lab.

Grace loved her massive lab that was basically an immense bright white tube-like structure that always smelt heavenly of freshly cut grass, jasmine and cinnamon buns. Her lab was filled with rows upon rows of white hovering workbenches where her and her students and lab techs would happily spend hours working on DNA, genetics and all the other wonderful biological problems they had to solve.

But it was all empty tonight.

There wasn't another soul in the lab and that was exactly how Grace wanted it. She didn't want to face anyone yet because she knew that everyone would shortly know what she had done.

In the Great Human Empire, it was illegal as hell to interact and free an alien. It was even more illegal not to report it to the authorities and Grace actually should have done a damn slight more if she wanted to keep her job.

She should have reported the missing engineering department and the station going off course as soon as she had discovered it.

The utter silence of the lab was peaceful and rather relaxing after listening to the foul laughter of the creature. Grace had actually done some extra research on the creature and they were real, humanity had been watching them for thousands of years in different ways and humanity admitted that they would never learn what they truly were.

Because where do you really begin if you want to understand how energy can live, think and interact with the material world?

Grace just knew she couldn't. But somehow someone had captured it and bound the creature to the station in some vain hope of something happening. In a strange way even though Grace was realising that the entire station and the thousands of lives on it (including her own) was nothing more than an experiment to see if the creature would kill them, she was rather glad she had gotten to be a part of it.

Because if the creature had never been captured then she wouldn't have learnt the truth about the station, and the computer systems never would have been taught how to run themselves. Something that still scared Grace a little.

Only a little though.

And Grace was still happy that the engineers were okay, well and a lot more social than they were before. Apparently the creature had taught them how to be better people and Grace was looking forward to listening to them sing karaoke later on.

And what Grace was really pleased about was the fact that they were still alive. To people who hadn't dated as many hot men as Grace did with such a wide range of jobs, hobbies and careers, that might have sounded stupid.

But Grace had learnt long ago that the Empire had no problem killing people who knew too much. Grace was just glad that the Empire trusted her enough not to spill the secrets of the creature and what had really kept the station going for so long.

And that is exactly what she would continue to do, because no one would believe her anyway. Hell, she still didn't know if she believed it herself.

Grace forced herself to take a deep breath of the amazing air and she just turned around and went out of the lab.

She was going to go down to the singing, dancing and clubbing crew of her station and join them. She had met and seen and dealt with crazy things today but that was okay because she had survived.

And in a harsh deadly galaxy, that was everything and there were still a lot more amazing wonderful mysteries to uncover in the biology of the galaxy. And Grace couldn't wait for a single second to uncover them.

Not a second at all.

AUTHOR OF AGENTS OF THE EMPEROR SERIES
CONNOR WHITELEY
SOCIALLY CRIMINAL
A SCIENCE FICTION MYSTERY SHORT STORY

SOCIALLY CRIMINAL

Justice Aisha Roar sat on her favourite cold, damp and sticky wooden bar stool in the messy Public House just off Main Street in the heart of the criminal underworld. The light was dark, scary and criminally good just how she liked it and the pub was thankfully filled with her favourite people tonight.

She sat towards the back like she always did and she pressed her black-armoured back against the sticky wooden walls that stunk of cheap alcohol, sex and sweat, just like how a good pub should smell. There were a few floating orbs of light swimming around against the dirty black ceiling providing just enough light, but it wasn't like anyone here actually wanted to see anyone's faces.

Everyone here was just here to drink, be merry and maybe have some random sex because it just felt good in the moment.

Aisha had always loved her time here and the constant background noise of people talking, laughing and shouting made her thinly smile. It was always great to be here after a long day of hunting down criminals and killing them because that was the law, but she always loved a good drink even more.

There was a brand-new wooden stage up at the front of the pub which Aisha really didn't like, because there was some hip-pop rubbish band from Earth playing there.

Aisha really didn't know what crime those fools had committed to end up in some junk bar like this one. The musicians were good, damn good so Aisha just couldn't understand whatsoever why these people wanted to play here.

They could easily get thousands of Rexes and then even more through tips if they played in the Spires, where the posh people lived. So maybe their crime was just stupidity and Aisha was half tempted to donate some of her money to them but she had already met her personal monthly quota of charity giving.

And she wouldn't want to get a foul reputation as a do-gooder. She actually shuddered at the very idea.

A cute young couple walked past her table, the woman looked okay wearing a very short black skirt, and the young man looked stunning in his tight jeans, shirt and boots. Hopefully both of them were in for a lucky night tonight, but Aisha was still alone.

Most of the Justices on the planet preferred to be alone because it was what their job required, each Justice was a law onto themselves and no one except the Glorious Rex himself on Earth could ever challenge their judgement.

It didn't make dating easy, it certainly made having a family impossible but Aisha still loved her job. It was her small way of helping to make the Imperium a better place with less freaks, criminals and alien scum in it.

"Lady Justice," a man said coming over to the table.

Aisha rolled her eyes. As much as she loved helping people, donating secretly to charities and making the Imperium a safer place, everyone knew never to disturb a Justice when they were drinking.

There might not have been a lot of social activity in the Imperium outside of work, watching fights and gambling, but drinking was a sacred activity of the Justices.

"I was hoping to have a moment of your time in exchange for this," the man said.

A small floating orb of light hovered over head and Aisha had a feeling that the owner of the pub was watching her, technically illegally but privacy was a joke these days.

Aisha focused on the small crystal glass of golden liquid and she instantly knew it was a very fine whiskey not found on this planet.

That had to have cost the man a few thousand Rexes, so why was he giving it to her?

Aisha looked at the man and he was surprisingly young with smooth sexy features, a pretty face and his slim body looked amazing in his tight robes denoting he was from the local College.

Definitely a man that did not belong in the deepest, darkest depths of this planet.

"Are there not Justices at the Colleges? In the Spires? In your own family?" Aisha asked.

The floating orb of light dipped a little lower and if it dared to get much closer then Aisha would happily smash it. What could the owner of the pub do? Call the Justices?

"Of course but I require a more roguish touch for my problem and I know you have a very effective reputation for getting rid of people," the man said.

Aisha had to admit she loved how her reputation was finally taking shape but she really didn't want this young man thinking that Justices were dangerous, it was the criminals they hunted that they were the real danger. Then she just smiled because the constant indoctrination that all subjects of the Imperium went through should take care of that.

"Of course, if your target has committed a crime then they will die. That is the law. If they steal a slice of bread, they die. If they assault someone, they die. If they murder someone, they die," Aisha said.

The young man frowned a little. "My wedding application got denied recently and I want you to fix it,"

Aisha smiled. It was a great effective feature of the Imperium that in order for two people to get married the Rex had to personally approve it and even then they could only get married if it served the Imperium.

A lot of maths, statistics and problem-solving was used to calculate how great the marriage would impact the Imperium and most of the time marriages were accepted. It was important to the fabric of society that the rich only married the rich, doctors only married doctors and the poor only married the poor. It was critical to stop the corrupting influence of the lower classes from ruining the rich people that were actually going to make something of themselves.

Aisha wasn't always sure she agreed with but it was an interesting idea.

"The Rex made his decision, even a Justice cannot overrule them. What were the stated reasons?" Aisha asked.

"I cannot marry my girlfriend because I am a student and she is a military Commander two years older than me,"

Aisha nodded. That was strange and it meant that the girlfriend had to come from a military family to get promoted that quickly. But students and military types were always marrying.

Except when one thing was revealed.

"What are you studying in?" Aisha asked.

The man smiled and Aisha smiled too. He was clearly passionate about it, so it had to be something grand like the military, sciences, medicine or a whole host of other brilliant subjects.

"I'm studying game design," the man said.

Aisha just reached across the table, grabbed the man's whiskey and downed it in one.

There was nothing kind she could say to the man because game design was useless to helping the Imperium survived so he was a useless man. But it was clear as day that he loved the subject.

And Aisha had always respected passion.

"And I refused to take the propaganda module," the man said.

Out of instinct Aisha moved her hand down to her waist where her gun was but she stopped her. This young man wasn't a radical that was a danger to the Imperium. He was just a young man that wanted to marry his girlfriend.

He did not need to die no matter how many of her peers would have killed him for not helping the Imperium indoctrinate young minds through games.

That was actually a crime so technically she had to kill this young man but she wanted to learn more and help him.

And if she found more evidence of his crimes against the Imperium then she would sadly have to kill him.

"I've come to you because the personal reference on my marriage application lied about me," the man said.

Aisha leant forward. Now that was a much more serious crime.

"What's your name?" Aisha asked as she stood up and downed the rest of her drink in one.

"Joshua Laurie," he said.

Aisha grabbed him and took him out of the pub. "Well Joshua, take me to this liar and then we will see how he committed the most outrageous crime imaginable. They lied to the Glorious Rex himself,"

Aisha felt so excited as they left the pub because she was finally going to hunt down her criminal.

A criminal that might need the ultimate punishment.

***

Aisha was hardly surprised too much when Joshua led her down through the dirty, stinky and toxic narrow streets of the criminal underworld with her fingers tightly on the trigger of her gun.

Then Joshua led her into a very crawl and dirty metal chamber inside an abandoned building. The chamber itself was immense covered with black mouldy walls, puddles of stagnant water covered the floor as did streaks of brown dried blood.

Aisha just smiled as she watched two very attractive middle-aged men clearing up after the fight that had caused the streaks of blood, and judging by the sheer amount of holo-cigars, bullets and broken weapons there must have been a hell of a crowd here tonight.

There were only three social activities in all of the Imperium. There was drinking which Aisha loved, there was watching or taking part in fights or there was gambling. Aisha really didn't like the last two because she preferred fighting on the streets (illegal to all but Justices) and gambling was just stupid.

But judging by the chamber some people seriously loved

watching a good fight.

"This is the man that lied on my application," Joshua said pointing to one of the two middle-aged men.

Aisha pointed her gun at him and just focused on how disgusting he looked in his dirty cloak, soaked-through boots and blackened teeth.

"Why the hell did you want this man on your wedding application?" Aisha asked.

"Because I'm his father," the man said.

Aisha just shook her head. There really was no ending to humanity's stupidity and it made no sense how this man working in the criminal underworld had managed to get a son into a local College. That should have been impossible.

Aisha made a note to herself to investigate the College tomorrow. There was no telling if Joshua's criminal family might have started corrupting the rich students of the College.

"Why did you lie dad on my application? I saw it and you said I was unfaithful to my girlfriend and I had donated to pro-Keres charities,"

Aisha pointed the gun at the son. The Keres were foul alien abominations that wanted to destroy humanity and their way of life. It was an awful crime to help them.

"Relax Lady Justice, he did no such thing," the father said.

Aisha decided to put her gun away because these two people made no sense and their actions literally went against how the Imperium worked.

"How are you two even related? There are strict laws against poor degenerates going to College. How did you get in?" Aisha asked.

Joshua smiled. "My girlfriend pulled a few strings and got me into college. I rose up through the class quickly and effectively and now I'm on the Student Council,"

As much as Aisha wanted to be annoyed that a poor person had a position of power in the local College, she actually couldn't be annoyed. The man was clearly intelligent, kind and passionate and of course Aisha would never admit this to her peers but the Imperium needed more people like that.

And so many of the laws were just dumb social laws to control others that it was just so stupid.

Poor people needed to go to College, get educated and help the Imperium, because the rich people were hardly doing an amazing job.

The father came over to Aisha. "Please don't arrest me and my son. We're good people, I provide innocent workers with sanctioned entertainment and that is what my son wants to do. We want to be entertainers, not criminals,"

All of Aisha's instincts, training and textbooks were telling her to just kill these two people now because they were a theoretical threat to the Imperium, but they weren't.

They seriously weren't.

Aisha knew that the father just wanted to entertain people as did the son just through different methods, but there was still one important question left.

"Why didn't you want your son getting married?" Aisha asked.

The father looked at the ground focusing on a long streak of blood that looked impossible to clean.

"I wanted my son to marry who he actually loves. He doesn't love the military girl, they both only wanted sex from each other and they were both using each other,"

Aisha looked at Joshua. "Is this true?"

Joshua nodded like he was proud of it. "Yeah. She wanted to have sex with a poor degenerate for the thrill and I wanted to go to College. I wanted her as much as she wanted me but when her father started asking questions she wanted to get married to protect herself,"

"And you didn't?" Aisha asked.

Joshua nodded and Aisha had to admit it was nice when the father hugged his son, that was a rare sight these days in the Imperium. A very unfortunate day.

As Aisha just looked at the father and son she couldn't deny how badly the law said they both had to die. The father had lied to the Rex himself, the son had illegally gone to College and used a military girl for his own gain (a strange little law made that illegal) and even the girlfriend needed to die technically because she had been having sex outside her permissible social rank.

It was all so stupid and as much as it would end Aisha's life, career and drinking fund if anyone found out she simply lowered her gun and walked away.

There were no crimes here, not real ones anyway, and all these social crimes were all victimless but Aisha still had to investigate the College just in case.

But she really, really hoped that Joshua would find happiness because it was the very least that everyone deserved.

***

Aisha had loved stalking the long perfectly clean, refreshingly nutty-scented air of the local College as she had investigated for any sign of corruption amongst the local rich students, and thankfully there had been none. In fact they seemed to be even more dedicated and indoctrinated into the Imperial Cult that worshipped everything the Rex said as divine law.

That was brilliant for the sake of the Imperium.

As Aisha sat later that night at the back of the bar again resting her black armour against the wooden sticky walls and her hands wrapped around a wonderfully cold tankard of beer, she was really happy with herself.

Because by proving that the law was wrong about the strict social controls of the Imperium, maybe she could get them to be dropped as laws and then the Rex's plans for mass indoctrination could be even stronger, better and more effective so no one could ever question the righteousness of his rule.

Then maybe there would be less criminals and that meant more drinking time in this great pub. Aisha really did enjoy the constant sweet aromas of sweat, stale beer and sex, there was just nothing else like it.

And in a cold, unloving galaxy, Aisha knew that love was always needed and now Joshua was alive and free to find who he loved and hopefully Aisha could find someone to love her in the end.

She smiled at that, that really would be an amazing thing to have.

But until then would always be more criminals, more murders and thieves to find, investigate and kill and that seriously excited Aisha a lot more than she ever wanted to admit.

AUTHOR OF AGENTS OF THE EMPEROR
CONNOR WHITELEY
LESSON IN GALAXY BURNING
A SCIENCE FICTION ADVENTURE SHORT STORY

LESSON IN GALAXY BURNING

Mother Siren Elizabeth Abec had always flat out loved the *Coming Of Age* celebrations on Akicus, because with the world being shrouded in eternal darkness, it meant the forces of the Lord of War would celebrate in style. Compared to the dull mundane Great Human Empire that she was so glad she was no longer a part of.

For seven Standard Days straight, the entire atmosphere of Akicus was covered in bright explosions, red and green and purple fireworks and the entire planet stunk of smoke.

Elizabeth leant against the icy cold copper railing of the gladiator Colosseum to see the great match that was about to unfold below her. And the entire reason why she had stepped away from her most holy duties to come to these celebrations in the name of her God, the almighty Lord of War.

She ran her fingers across the railing. It was finely crafted, there wasn't a chip, dent or any sign that this railing, like much of the massive grey stone Colosseum was over three thousand years old. Maybe the people of Akicus did actually know a thing or two about other topics besides murder, bloodshed and war.

Only maybe.

But she was here today to save herself, her friends and her Sisterhood.

She carefully placed her large crystal glass of bloodred champagne on the railing. The champagne smelt surprisingly good with its strong hints of fruit, iron and a little shot of blood. The blood was meant to help the drinker adopt the traits and skills of the victim, but she had never brought such claims.

Elizabeth couldn't deny her husband would have loved the Colosseum. Its triangular design was impressive as the structure rose up for hundreds of kilometres allowing for millions upon millions of bloodthirsty watchers to sit in long rows and watch for the mindless murder to start.

She noticed at the top of every triangular part of the Colosseum was a VIP metal box like hers. Each box contained small engines, shields and everything she needed to escape if there was an attack or not. Of course the poor innocent watchers below did not get those luxuries.

The Governor of Akicus probably wanted them all to die. That was the goal of the Galaxy Burners after all. A mindless murderous legion of superhumans dedicated to exterminating all life from the galaxy.

This was one of their recruiting worlds.

Elizabeth raised her champagne glass to some of the Great Houses of the world who were looking at her from the two other boxes. Their long sweeping red, white and ocean blue robes were attractive and their large golden necklaces certainly proved their point about them being nobles and powerful.

But Elizabeth was so much more powerful than them and she loved it. She liked having the power to summon entire legions, bombardments and she could melt this world if she wanted to. All because she was a Siren, a prophet of the Lord of War in the eyes of the other legions.

That gave her all the power needed, and Elizabeth just smiled as some of the nobles started drinking more bloodred champagne in an effort to get the traits of the victim. Maybe the nobles believed they could defeat her with their stupid claims.

It was simply the people of Arkcius falling to her sisterhood's lies, deceit and mind games.

Elizabeth had served the Sirens of Ares for almost three

thousand years now and she had loved every day. She had loved the scheming, killing and launching their holy war against the corrupt, foul Human Empire that was way too weak to rule humanity. Humanity needed to be ruled with an iron fist, strict laws and mass genocides for anyone who dared to defy the Lord of War.

The Empire was not about those ideals, so they were weak and pathetic and doomed to die.

And Elizabeth hoped that her being here today to watch a very special contestant would help the Empire die just a little sooner.

"Mother Siren," a small woman said in the bright metallic blue armour of her legion, "it is an honour to be allowed to watch the games with you,"

"Thank you for agreeing to come Novice,"

Elizabeth supposed she wasn't exactly meant to talk to Novices because she outranked them so highly that Novices were basically ants compared to her, but even ants can be extremely useful on days like this.

Captain Maxis Gates on paper was your typical Galaxy Burners Captain. He did not care about life, he only enjoyed killing and his greatest delight was making the streets of a world run thick with blood. He was exactly what every Galaxy Burner was meant to be.

Yet in reality, he had a very rare quality amongst his legion. He was able to resist The Rage. At first Elizabeth had suggested the Rage was some lame excuse the Burners had come up with to explain away from their murderous intent, but no, they actually had a psychological flaw implanted in their DNA.

When Doctor Catherine Taylor had created each superhuman legion from scratch, she had chosen to put a psychological flaw inside the Burners' DNA that meant the only emotion they could feel was rage, and the rage became a focus for more. So the more they killed, the more rage they experienced and they wanted to experience an emotion for once in their life.

And people say the Lord of War is cruel.

"Mother Siren, forgive me for speaking but I still do not

understand why we are here. We are Sisters, we are not Burners,"

Elizabeth nodded. "Of course but you are being so small-minded Novice. It is our duty to find out talent within the legions and make a decision to serve our Legion Lord. If a person is a threat to the Sisterhood then they must die,"

She took a sip of the wonderful champagne, and it was an explosion of flavour in her mouth. The rich hints of oranges, grapefruit and the crispiness of the bubbles were amazing and the little pop from the blood just brought the flavour all together.

It was perfect.

"Ladies and Gentleman," the Planetary Governor shouted and continued.

Elizabeth placed her hand carefully on her superhuman gun, capable of exploding heads with a single bullet, at her waist. She knew the Governor was three hundred kilometres below her but she felt safer with her gun in her fingers.

The Governor was no fan of the Sisterhood, thankfully his opinion mattered little.

"Today Maxis will become a Commander if he proves himself worthy," the Governor said.

"That is why we are here," the Novice said.

"Yes," Elizabeth said. "Maxis will have to face three challenges and if he survives then I will have enough information to make my judgement,"

"Why not just kill him now Mother Siren?"

Elizabeth laughed. That wasn't a bad point. The main benefit of the Rage was that it meant the Burners were easy to control, they would roll over like dogs as long as you gave them another battle and another chance to kill people. Yet if Maxis was proof that the Rage could be cured then that might make the Burners harder to control.

And the Lord of War might have to cure them or face the Burners in a civil war. Not something Elizabeth wanted to test in the slightest.

"Just watch," Elizabeth said picking up her champagne glass.

Inside the gladiator pit, there was a small bare-chested superhuman man with a perfectly muscular powerful body capable of ripping humans and aliens and mutants limb from limb without a second thought. His face was burnt and sacred and he was smiling.

It was the sort of smile that a predator gave a victim before it died in the worst way possible.

Maxis didn't even have a sword, a gun or anything. He only had his bare fists.

Three massive black-furred wolves appeared, the size of houses and they snarled. The crowd broke out in a scream and deafening cheers.

The wolves charged and Elizabeth had to admit she was impressed with Maxis.

The wolves striked as one but it didn't matter. The wolves were a second behind each other. More than enough time for a superhuman to react.

Maxis leapt into the air, spun around and he landed with a punch on the wolf's spine. A deafening crack echoed all around the Colosseum and the crowd again crowd out in extreme euphoria.

They were more than happy at the death.

The second and third wolves didn't even slow down for their dead friend. They leapt. They clawed. They slashed at Maxis.

Not that it mattered much.

Maxis gripped one of the immense claws and broke it over his knee like it was made of cheap plastic. And then he simply rammed it into the wolves' skulls at the same time so both died instantly.

Elizabeth leant on the railing even more and she couldn't help noticing that Maxis appeared fine. There were no signs of rage, no signs of transformation and no signs that he was finding the kill a challenge.

This must have been child's play to him.

Maybe the rumours were true about him being immune to the Rage.

"Novice, I need a favour," Elizabeth said as the crowd screamed in utter euphoria at the glorious death around them. "I need you to contact Beastmaster Holden and request a Blood Dragon for the final event on the authority of the Lord of War,"

The Novice's eyes blinked like Elizabeth had punched her in the face. Clearly the Novice had never had the privilege to use their faith to their manipulative advantage before.

Now the Novice was going to learn just how powerful the Sisterhood could be in the shadows.

"Of course Mother Siren," the Novice said leaving.

Elizabeth shrugged. She was never going to see the little Novice again because to create a Blood Dragon required a holy sacrifice. Oh well.

By the time the Novice had left the metal viewing platform, the next event had started. Elizabeth just took her head at the deafening roar of exploding red and bronze fireworks, the euphoric crowd and the smashing of swords down in the pit.

Twenty men, clearly infused with steroids, were fighting, slashing and slicing at Maxis to no avail.

Maxis painted the sand red, made the dark red rich blood flood into the sand making it sticky and muddy and the victims screamed out in agony as Maxis shattered bones.

Elizabeth took another sip of the wonderfully refreshing champagne and she had to admit Maxis was a hell of a fighter. He would be a good weapon against the Empire, and he could burn a lot of Empire worlds for them.

But he hated the Sisterhood, and that meant he was a threat.

Not a lot of people knew this in the Confederacy, but the Sisterhood had spies, eyes and ears everywhere. It was not hard to find out that Maxis had been coordinating across the legions to create secret meetings to discuss the ending and extermination of the Sisterhood.

Elizabeth's hands formed fists. It was so disgusting, outrageous and foul that Maxis was plotting to murder so many of her kin. Each sister was a brave, courageous and helpful soldier that only wanted to serve the Lord of War so humanity could be better off under his iron grip. They never ever deserved to die.

So Maxis was going to have to die instead and the Sisterhood would recover his DNA in time and see if the Rage could be cured or manipulated. If they found the genetic key to the Rage then maybe they could corrupt other humans.

That would be a fun idea.

"And for our final event ladies and gentlemen," the Governor said, "we have a special event requested by the Sisterhood itself. Now let's kill this creature like we will one day kill the Sisterhood,"

Elizabeth smiled. The Governor was a fat old fool for sure, and he had certainly outlived his usefulness. She didn't even think the Burners would mind him dying considering he was a mere figurehead for the Burners' recruitment operations on the planet.

Out of the massive blood-soaked sandy pit, a large metallic bloodred dragon grew out of the sand. Its scales were made from steel, its eyes were as bright as starship engines and his metallic tongue licked the air. It was wonderful what the Confederacy had access to after a while of raiding planets.

The dragons zoomed forwards and Maxis was a great fighter but there was a reason why she had picked this creature as the final event.

Maxis slashed, smashed and lashed at the dragon as he rolled again and again to avoid the torrents of fire. Maxis smashed the twenty swords and claws from the past rounds into the dragon.

The dragon kept breathing fire and Maxis screamed and hissed out in pain.

The air tasted of blood and iron and smoke as the sand smouldered and turned to molten glass. Maxis ran into the glass by mistake, he screamed bloody murder and cried out in agony.

Even his superhuman biology couldn't cope with what was happening. Still the dragon kept coming and attacking and Maxis never stopped attacking either.

He threw a sword straight into the dragon's eyes and then it happened.

Elizabeth finished her wonderfully refreshing champagne as the dragon roared a final time and all euphoria in the crowd was lost. The crowd stopped talking, shouting and cheering and a wave of silence washed over them.

The dragon glowed bright red and piercing bright golden light poured out of the gaps in-between its scales. And a massive golden shockwave pulsed out of it.

Maxis collapsed to the ground but he shook and got back up. He roared like a monster and a chill ran down Elizabeth's spine at the sheer inhumanness of it.

Elizabeth shook slightly at the sight of Maxis growing even taller, so he was twelve metres tall, his hands and fingers became tentacles and his entire body transformed into the most terrifying thing she had ever seen. This was not a superhuman anymore, this was not a mortal human anymore, this was something else.

Maxis shot forward and ripped the dragon limb from limb and Elizabeth nodded. This was the Rage fully exposed, this was what all Burners were capable of and if all it took was for a Dragon to unleash their inner darkness then she might have just discovered a brand new weapon.

And a beautiful brand-new weapon at that.

Maxis ripped chunks out of the metallic dragon even after it was dead.

It was clear that the creature wanted more blood, more war and more everything. It was feeling emotion constantly for the first time in its life and Elizabeth simply licked her lips because her mission was complete.

She had found a way to silence her critics and save her Sisterhood and most importantly she had discovered a much better way at destroying the Burners. If a Burner ever posed her Sisterhood a threat again then she would only need to unleash the power of a Blood Dragon against them to unlock their DNA's full potential.

And this would send a clear message to her enemies in the Confederacy. If anyone messed with the Sisterhood then they were going to die in one way or another, because no one would follow or believe what Maxis had to say now.

He couldn't even speak bless him. He could only roar, scream and chomp on flesh so he could keep feeling emotions that he had never had the pleasure of experiencing before.

Elizabeth raised her empty glass to the nobles of the Great Houses in the other metal boxes as they were still looking at her. Their faces made her smile because they were so scared, so afraid and so intimidated by her because they had learnt maybe for the first time in their lives that all the power they had was simply an illusion.

No one had power in the confederacy, not the senate, not the nobles, not even the planetary governors. The only person with power in the confederacy were the superhuman Angels of Death and Hope.

And the Sisterhood was one of the most powerful of them all.

A fact that made Elizabeth very, very happy indeed.

AUTHOR OF AGENTS OF THE EMPEROR
CONNOR WHITELEY
ART IN THE SEEING
A SCIENCE FICTION SPACE OPERA SHORT STORY

ART IN THE SEEING

Professor Leilani Nutter had always loved, more than anything else in the entire Empire, studying ancient objects made, forged and created by alien civilisations. Sure some of the objects that came through her large bright white lab were a little tacky, others were small and unimpressive but every so often a truly amazing find came through her lab.

Leilani stood in the very centre of her very large bright white lab with its beautiful smooth white walls, that weren't a cold sort of white that made chills run down her spine. Instead the walls were a sort of warming and almost welcoming shade of white that still sent the message to the others that they were entering a highly professional and sterile clean lab environment, but this wasn't a cold awful place like a lot of other university labs.

Leilani just smiled at that because this wasn't even a part of one of the Empire's millions of universities. Her lab was extremely high up in the Nepalese mountains buried deep within the Empire Palace and Leilani just got more and more excited each day because she just knew that somewhere high above her was the Emperor of The Great Human Empire walking about.

And Leilani truly had no idea if she would cry, scream or faint if she actually ever had the pleasure of meeting the hero of humanity.

The lab's dark blue floor was a particular favourite of Leilani's with its heat-sensitive array that made sure the lab was always the perfect mixture of oxygen, nitrogen and humidity to make sure all her staff were perfectly okay and alert, and each of the artifacts and other things that came through the lab were in perfect condition.

Damaging any of the objects gifted or loaned to her was the very last thing she ever wanted to do.

Leilani really loved the amazing smell of crispness, freshness and nature that the dark blue floor created for the lab. She had worked in far too many academic labs over her life and she had hated the musky, dusty smell of those labs, but her one thankfully smelt heavenly.

She seriously loved her lab. Especially as the refreshing air reminded her of the taste of sausages, burgers and fish from family camping holidays in the now-long-dead woods and forests of ancient Earth when she was a kid all those centuries ago.

Even the light sky-blue ceiling was an impressive array that Leilani had been more than happy to shell out some of her own money for, because the ceiling was filled with microscopic sensors, cameras and other highly sought-after equipment that was always monitoring everything so the lab never ever missed a detail from an artifact or piece or art or whatever came through the lab.

Leilani was still surprised at how much that had saved her over the years. There was one time when she had received a tiny fragment of an alien's skull and for some reason when it first entered the lab it started transmitting data to somewhere in deep, deep space.

Leilani would have missed all of that data completely if it hadn't of been for the ceiling's equipment, Leilani just loved her lab more than anything else in the entire world.

The talking, muttering and academic discussions of her staff in their sterile white lab coats walked past her as each of them got on with their own projects. And thankfully her two favourite undergraduates had just bought her the latest gift from the Emperor.

Apparently it was a work of art.

Thankfully the very large bright white lab had plenty of grey metal work benches scattered neatly around the lab so large groups and pairs of staff were mostly gathered about them working on their own things.

Leilani loved how each member of her staff had massive smiles on their faces, they were all happy to be here and they all truly did believe that their work mattered. And in a way it did because the discoveries they made here could very well determine the fate of humanity and the course the Empire took.

It was Leilani's lab that allowed the Empire to make Slidspace jumps so no one needed to travel at sublight speeds. It was Leilani's lab that allowed the Empire in the very early days of space travel and the Emperor to create shields and dampers and everything thing else that humanity needed to travel into deep space. And it was Leilani herself that had worked with Doctor Catherine Taylor on creating the superhuman soldiers of the Angels of Death and Hope.

Their work definitely mattered.

Right in front of Leilani was a large wooden box on a grey metal hovering bench as she carefully ran her fingers along the coldness of the wooden box.

The box hummed, crackled and whirled a little as the wooden dissolved away revealing an extremely stunning work of art.

Leilani was just flat out amazed as she stared at a large golden metal bowl, easily the size of a small child, with a perfectly smooth interior so Leilani could easily see her own reflection, something she rarely saw in alien objects these days, and the outside was even more beautiful.

The outside of the golden metal bowl was covered in stunning diamonds, rubies and sapphires embedded into the thin metal of the bowl, but Leilani just knew that the gems were arranged into a special pattern.

To others the gemstones just looked beautiful as they all reflected the bright white light of the lab perfectly, and almost created a kind of kaleidoscopic effect on the ceiling. But to Leilani, the diamonds were arranged in a very certain way as were the rubies and rich dark sapphires.

It didn't take Leilani long to work out the pattern and she was surprised that it was a language of sorts, so she was really looking forward to running that through the supercomputers and checking her textbooks to try and narrow down the language that it was.

The entire bowl seemed so mystical to Leilani and it was nothing like she had ever seen before, it wasn't that she hadn't studied bowls before, she had, a lot more than once. But this bowl just felt special to her like the creator of the bowl had literally poured their heart and soul into the creation.

And there was something Leilani really wanted to honour about that.

"Is this the shipment professor?" a young woman said.

Leilani looked at the young woman standing on the opposite side of the hovering grey metal bench and Leilani just smiled as she was really glad to have one of her best PhD students with her.

Laura Coleman had to be one of the sharpest minds that Leilani had ever had the pleasure of working with, she wasn't perfect and Leilani was glad to still know a lot more about the galaxy than Laura, but Laura might honestly be able to run this lab in a few decades, and Leilani was actually looking forward to that if Laura just kept learning, studying and helping the Empire to advance.

And Leilani had to admit she looked good in her long white silk robe, white high-heels and her very long brown hair managed to accent the entire look in a rather stunning way. She wasn't beautiful because Leilani really preferred guys, but she could understand why Laura was so popular with the male graduates.

"Yes," Leilani said, returning her focus to the stunning golden bowl in front of her. "It came the Galactic North on the Frontier earlier and it was given an Empire Decree to jump the queue,"

"Why would the Emperor want this bowl studied so quickly? Does he forget how massive our backlist is? I'm still studying objects that came in before my undergrad degree,"

"Which one?" Leilani asked smiling.

Laura poked her tongue out and that was something else that Leilani really loved about helping to train the next generation of researchers, they all had such a fun, positive outlook on life. And that was something Leilani seriously treasured.

Leilani watched Laura get out a thin black dataslate as Leilani put on her white gloves and carefully ran her long fingers across the inside of the bowl.

A minor pulse of energy travelled up her arm and she was surprised that it felt curious than anything else. It wasn't unfriendly, evil or even happy. It was only curious.

"Ceiling equipment says there's a lot of energy inside this bowl," Laura said showing Leilani the readings.

Leilani was surprised to see the sheer amount of power the equipment was detecting inside the bowl. It was like nothing she had ever seen before, it was like the entire bowl had enough power to destroy the entire Empire Palace if it really wanted to.

It made no sense that a mere bowl would contain this much power.

"Do you recognise the language?" Leilani asked. Even if Laura didn't know the exact language she might be able to at least give Leilani a starting point.

"No sorry," Laura said.

Leilani smiled. It was worth a shot and there weren't that many ancient alien cultures that used gemstones to communicate, and as it was found in the galactic North and that was the area humanity knew most about, it shouldn't be too difficult to find out more.

But the energy was still puzzling Leilani.

"What if you search the archive, professor?" Laura asked.

It wasn't a bad idea and all Leilani would need to do was run a quick scan of the bowl and then the computers would conduct a sort of image scan in case they had investigated such an artifact or language before.

"Good idea, can you do it?" Leilani asked as she got closer to the bowl, so close she could smell the bowl.

Leilani heard Laura softly laugh at her, but Leilani didn't mind and she had to admit she had to look weird as she carefully sniffed the golden bowl.

And she was right, the air around the bowl didn't smell metallic at all. It actually smelt of charred flesh, burnt ozone and even a little blood.

Leilani gestured for Laura to pass her over the black dataslate, and Leilani quickly tested for traces of blood in the bowl.

A very dark orange light passed over the golden bowl for about five seconds.

"Here," Leilani said showing Laura the results. "DNA and blood from twenty different species have been identified over the course of about two hundred years,"

Laura's mouth dropped and after a few moments Leilani completely agreed. It was bad enough that the Emperor himself had felt the need to get involved once this object was discovered, but it was even weirder that they had discovered a sacrificial bowl.

In the grand scheme of things so few alien cultures even used sacrifices even in their earliest days, it seemed to be a very rare event in the development of other cultures that was mostly limited to humanity, and why had the golden bowl only been used for two hundred years?

To other people that might have sounded like a very long time for an object to still be around and it really was. But Leilani just felt like there was more to the story.

And why did a sacrificial bowl have so much energy built up inside it?

The dataslate vibrated slightly in Leilani's hands as the results of Laura's archive search came back. Laura took the dataslate back from Leilani.

"The results show," Laura said, "that we have never looked at an object with this gemstone language but there is a passing similarity to an object from the… sorry how do you pronounce that?"

Leilani smiled as she looked at the dataslates screen. "The Atooch Culture,"

Laura shrugged at the name of the culture and Leilani was rather surprised she hadn't come across it, considering Laura was doing her PhD on cultures and alien civilisations in the central regions of the milky way galaxy, she really should have known it.

"The Atooch Culture," Leilani said, "was a hunter gatherer culture that went from planet to planet in the galactic centre for about a thousand years before it died off. They weren't religious, they didn't believe in war, they only believed in survival,"

And as she said that she was even more surprised that they used gemstones in fact because the Atooch Culture didn't believe in material property too much. Their focus was literally on survival.

"The culture did have a language of sorts and we've managed to unpick most of it and I guess it has some similarity to the gemstones but not a lot,"

"So why did the Archive search link the two?" Laura asked.

Leilani clicked her fingers as she knelt down on the perfectly comfortably warm dark blue floor and she truly focused on the gemstones. She stared at the bright sparkling diamonds.

After a few seconds the diamonds started to blink, flash and started to do something. It showed her ancient words in languages she did recognise and when the scan was being done the equipment must have recorded all of this hence the results of the image search.

But Leilani was only seeing it now. "The object is saying something about… *blood gives the seeker to power to see,"*

Leilani had absolutely no idea what it meant but if the amazing Emperor had wanted *her* to research it then she just knew that he wanted her to do something special.

Because if Leilani had learnt one thing from Doctor Catherine Taylor, a real legend in Empire science it was that sometimes the rules and laws and regulations controlling her lab had to be ignored.

"Do we still have those emergency blood bags in the medical room?" Leilani asked.

Laura looked up at the ceiling for a few moments and nodded.

"Good, please get me one," Leilani said as she watched Laura walk off.

If her suspicions were correct then Leilani wouldn't have been surprised if this bowl did have some kind of power or ability of its own. A power that had been gifted to the bowl by its alien creators all those hundreds of thousands of years ago.

A few moments later Laura thankfully came out holding a small sealed plastic bag filled with blood and the entire shape of the bag reminded her of a joint of beef before it was cooked.

It was only about two litres but if there was ever a mishap in the lab then that was normally more than enough to help the poor person.

And more often than not that poor person was Leilani.

Leilani carefully tapped the plastic bag as she held it over the golden bowl and she could feel some kind of energy pulse and radiate from the bowl.

She tapped the plastic bag one more time and the plastic dissolved. The dark red rich blood poured out of the bag and landed gently into the golden bowl.

The blood settled perfectly in the bowl like it had been designed for each other.

"Now what?" Laura asked.

Leilani wasn't sure but her stomach just twisted into a painful knot as she was really questioning how wise this actually was.

"Maybe you need to see what you want to seek?" Laura asked.

Leilani nodded. That was a good idea. "Show me my homeworld,"

Nothing happened.

Leilani just rolled her eyes, maybe the bowl didn't work after all and maybe this bowl was just that, a mere bowl.

Then the blood bubbled a still and changed to reveal a perfect image of Earth floating in the cold void of space with millions of blade-like warships, fighters and cruisers coming and going. Exactly like how Earth was meant to be.

"Show me what I seek most in my life," Laura said.

Leilani was about to tell her off for daring to interfere with an artifact that she was examining because the bowl might not have liked having two speakers ask it things at the same time but that didn't seem to happen.

The image in the bowl changed to reveal something far darker as the image showed a very dark rocky cave in the middle of nowhere with a corpse inside it. Leilani instantly recognised it as her own.

Then the image revealed Laura was standing in the cave holding a knife that was dripping with Leilani's own blood.

"Show me exactly why I die?" Leilani asked.

The image didn't move, change or even bubble. The image wanted Leilani to know exactly that she was doomed to die on some forgotten planet by Laura's hand.

Laura just frowned at Leilani and Leilani really hoped that the future could be changed.

"Can the future be changed?" Leilani asked.

The image changed to reveal an ancient word that thankfully Leilani just knew meant yes but as she heard the very heavy footsteps of metal superhuman boots against the dark blue floor of her lab, she just knew that the Emperor had come to see her.

And right now she was much more interested in that visit than her own potential death.

Because it was about time the Emperor finally told her what the hell was going on.

***

As Leilani peacefully watched the immense golden armoured warriors of the Emperor's Guards with their massive golden crackling spears march Laura out of the bright white lab, Leilani just knew Laura was never ever going to be seen again. And judging by the panicked looks on the smooth and rough faces of her young and older staff, everyone else was realising that too.

But Leilani didn't feel like any of them particularly cared and in a strange way Leilani didn't either.

As Leilani moved to the other side of the grey metal hovering bench with the immensely impressively golden bowl filled with blood on it, she just couldn't understand why Laura had wanted to kill her in the present and in the future.

But she eventually understood it as the subtle hints of charred flesh, burnt ozone and metallic blood from the golden bowl hit her, it was all simply down to jealousy and Leilani really understood that. Laura had been trained by one of the top schools in the entire Empire, a place where it was expected that students were dumb sheep instead of being trained equals that were respected, admired and encouraged by teachers like Leilani.

Leilani had always made sure her students knew that they were loved and supported by her, but others in the Empire didn't agree with that sort of teaching. And Leilani had little doubt someone in the politics of Empire education had wanted to get rid of Leilani and her lab permanently and maybe they promised Laura the job too.

But that was all just good (and probably extremely accurate) speculation, and no good scientist bases their "facts" on speculation, but Leilani would never dare share those ideas with anyone.

The sheer silence of the lab made Leilani realise that the Emperor was still in the lab with them and everyone was too stunned into silence to speak.

Leilani was about to greet the Emperor but as soon as she really looked at this amazing, stunning three metre tall giant with thick ornate battle armour based on the armour of medieval knights from Ancient Earth, she was just stunned into silence. The sheer aura of power, respect and authority that radiated off him was so extreme that Leilani just had the urge to bow.

So she did and everyone else followed her.

When she stood back up perfectly straight, she looked at the Emperor's face and a sharp vibration radiated through her entire body. She had never seen anyone so beautiful, young and amazing like the Emperor before. He clearly wasn't naturally young but he was so beautiful and Leilani felt an immense wave of pride wash over her.

Like she was extremely proud of all a sudden to actually be a human and a citizen of the Empire. Because that's exactly what she was.

"My Lord," Leilani said, when her voice finally recovered. "It is an honour,"

"Relax," the Emperor said in such a caring and seductive voice that Leilani shivered with excitement.

The Emperor stepped towards the golden bowl. "I am impressive Professor Nutter, your achievements are quite something because no other species has ever been able to make these bowls work before,"

"Bowls?" Leilani asked.

The Emperor gestured her to come closer but Leilani was unsure and still had to force herself to get even closer to the God amongst men that was in front of her.

The Emperor waved his hand over the golden bowl and the image within it changed, showing a full scale picture of the Milky Way Galaxy but there were ten bright red dots on it.

"Each dot represents the location of another bowl. Some are in the hands of criminals and warlords, others are in the hand of the Empire, and more still are in the hands of the traitors," the Emperor said so matter-of-factly that Leilani felt her blood run cold.

Leilani just couldn't believe what she was hearing, if this was all true (and the Emperor was saying it so it just had to be) then this was simply awful. These bowls could tell and show the Seeker whatever they wanted, that sort of power would be horrific in the hands of bad people.

Leilani then noticed the Emperor was truly smiling at her, it wasn't a mocking smile or anything like that. It was a true, warm smile like a best friend might give to their own.

"And now you see why this had to be researched now," the Emperor said. "I needed to know if the bowls could be used at all by anyone, let alone the Traitor and Criminal forces. I do thank you for your service,"

Leilani bowed her head slightly and she simply stared into the dark rich red blood in the golden bowl. "Show me where this hunt to recover the bowls ends,"

The Emperor's smile deepened and Leilani was surprised that he allowed her to ask another question but he clearly wanted to know as well.

But the bowl simply bubbled and revealed no image.

"The future is unwritten," the Emperor said plainly. "I have much to do. Thank you everyone and especially you, Leilani,"

Leilani bowed her head a final time and as she listened to the warm heavy footsteps from the Emperor as he left the bright white lab, Leilani could feel everyone's gaze just look at her.

Everyone in the entire lab just knew the sheer power of these golden bowls and why they had to be completely recovered, because if the traitors were clever (and sadly they were) Leilani had little doubt they could be used to see Empire attack forces long before they reached the traitors, and the traitors would be able to counter every single attack made against them.

And that would cause so many deaths that Leilani seriously didn't want to even think about it.

So as everyone took a few steps towards Leilani with their smiles large and almost splitting their face, Leilani just knew that her amazing staff was right. There was a lot of learning, studying and researching to be if they were going to save the Empire.

And as Leilani set to work, she felt her stomach fill with butterflies because this was exactly where she needed to be and she was so excited to be doing exactly what she loved in the name of the Empire, Emperor and most importantly the Empire's amazing innocent people.

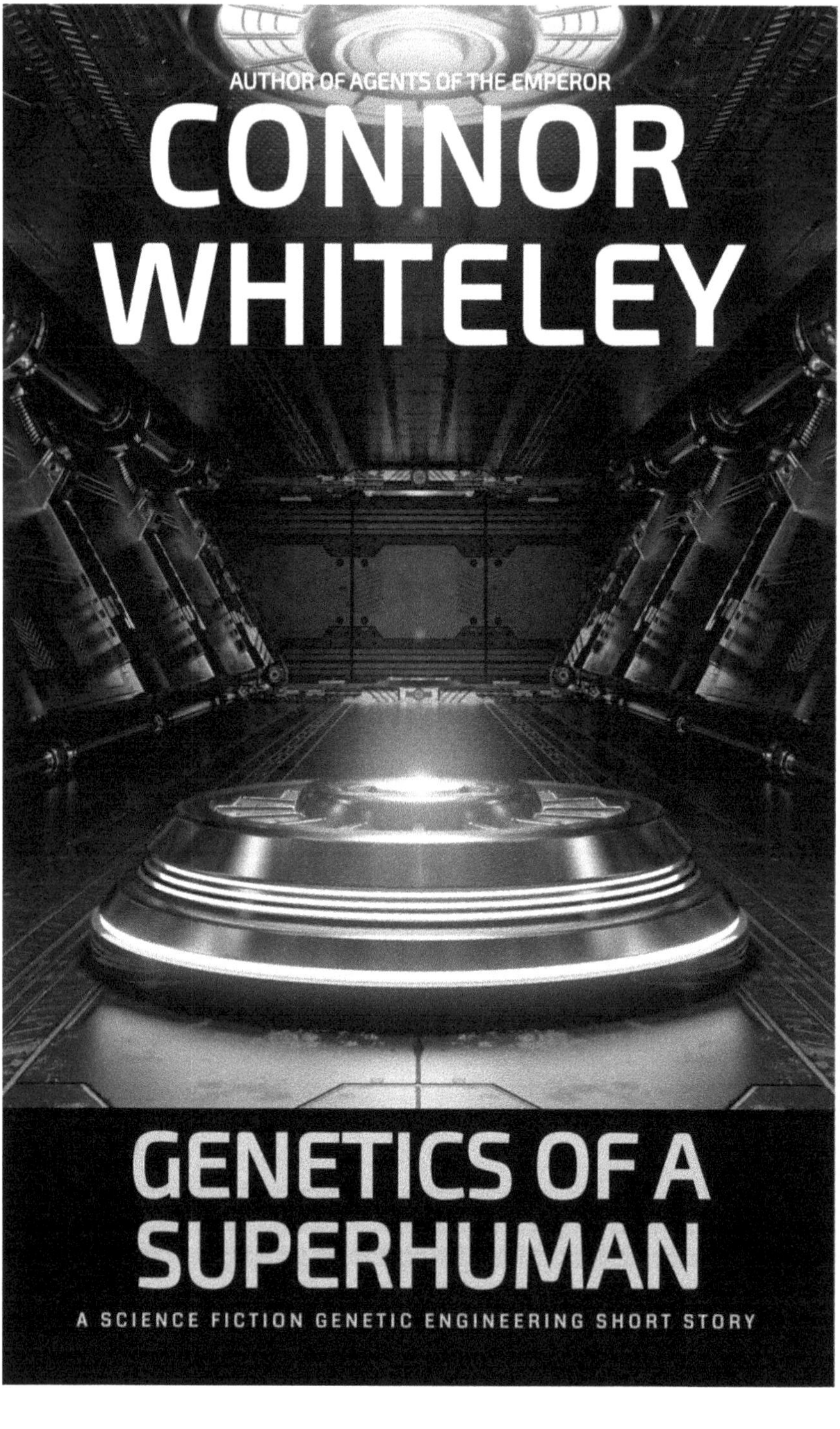
AUTHOR OF AGENTS OF THE EMPEROR
CONNOR
WHITELEY
GENETICS OF A
SUPERHUMAN
A SCIENCE FICTION GENETIC ENGINEERING SHORT STORY

GENETICS OF A SUPERHUMAN

It might have been over 90,000 years since Doctor Catherine Taylor had returned to the birthcradle of humanity, Earth, but she was more than glad to see it had changed. The very worst thing that humanity could ever allow itself to indulge in was stagnation.

Of course, she wouldn't have been surprised that the Emperor of The Great Human Empire never ever would have allowed that to happen. It was why she really, really liked him. He was so calm, wonderful and the best leader humanity had ever had.

And like her, the Emperor knew exactly the dangers posed by the traitor, alien and mutant that lurked in the deadly dark corners of the galaxy, just waiting for humanity to drop its guard and then they would slaughter humanity.

Catherine smiled to herself as she stood at the very edge of a massive metal hovering platform that was a perfect circle. Even by the standards of the Empire, it was next to impossible to find workmanship this perfect and ideal. But maybe that only showed how long she had been away from Earth and the beating heart of humanity.

The platform itself was nice enough. Catherine would have preferred to land her own blade-like warship on the platform but that had been denied firmly by the Emperor himself.

Every so often the platform pulsed, popped and vibrated. Catherine wouldn't have been surprised if the platform was scanning her or something because even after all these tens of thousands of years (and a lot more rejuvenation treatments than was probably healthy), Catherine still didn't know if the Emperor trusted her completely.

It was amazing what the running of so-called genetic experiments could do to a friendship that had been forged and maintained in the fires of war, betrayal and murder. Catherine didn't blame the Emperor at all, in fact she only loved him even more because of it.

Catherine watched as below the platform there were tens upon tens of immense lines of flying grey blade-like shuttles and warships and cruisers. They were constantly flowing in and out of the capital and Empire Government buildings.

She supposed that if a brand-new person had come to Earth then maybe they would be stupid enough to believe something major was happening. It wasn't. Earth was just as busy now as it always was because even though the lies reported on Empire media brainwashed humanity, Catherine knew the truth.

And the truth was simple. The noose was tightening around humanity's little narrow throat.

Catherine focused on the top-secret black blade-like shuttles belonging to the assassins. They looked to be out in force today and Catherine just grinned. There were always traitors, murderers and enemies on Earth that needed to be killed.

She was almost surprised that she hadn't been killed all those thousands of years ago. Apparently it was only the Emperor's love for her that had saved her, and Catherine was more than happy for that.

"Doctor," a man said behind her.

Catherine turned around and grinned as she saw an immense three-metre-tall superhuman man standing there in the fiery red armour of the Ignis Legion. He had his helmet up and that was why she was here, it was why she had raced back to Earth as soon as the Emperor had summoned her.

There was a problem with the superhuman Angels of Death and

Hope.

There was a problem with her children, her creations, her babies.

The man made the air smell of watermelon, mint and coconut, making the great taste of ice cream form on her tongue. Yet Catherine supposed this was simply part of the problem that she was meant to solve.

Catherine just focused on the warrior and couldn't immediately understand what was so wrong with him. Everything looked to be perfectly okay.

If there was a problem with the Angel's vestibular system then his balance would have been off, but he was fine. If the Angel had a problem with his breathing or superhuman organs then it would have shown. She would have been able to hear it.

But everything was fine.

Catherine realised that everything was too fine so she gestured the Angel to take off his helmet and she frowned.

She fully understood that she had never been the most emotional or involved or caring person in the Empire, but even she hated what had happened to her precious creations.

She had designed the Angels to be cold, calculating killers that would rip through the enemies of the Empire with ease. Yet she had designed them to look friendly, kind and very human at the same time but the face that was looking at her was no human.

The Angel's cheeks were hallowed, rotten and his eyes were like hardboiled eggs. Even the Angel's horrible tongue looked burnt, blistered and snake-like. It was awful.

Catherine wanted to kill this Angel as an affront to what was happening to her precious creations but if the Emperor had contacted her, then this was something that needed to be fixed at the genetic level. Maybe the Empire had already tried to contain the genetic problems by killing the faulty Angels.

It hadn't worked.

"Doctor," the man said and somehow managed to look her in the eye. Catherine was impressed.

"I will help you my child," Catherine said. "Just tell me what happened because I have been kept in the dark,"

"Two years ago the first group of Angels devolved like this. At first it was simple cosmetic problems but then it transformed into psychological difficulties. Entire squads of superhumans rebelling against their commanding officers. Killing entire villages and becoming mindless berserkers,"

Catherine nodded like she had heard it all before. She had no idea how her precious creations could end up like this but it was fascinating from a genetic standpoint. Maybe some of the genes had become so unstable that it was causing behavioural problems.

"Then two months ago the genetic problems were identified in every single Angel in the Empire and probably the traitors too," the man said.

Catherine laughed. Now that was really interesting because it was clear this wasn't an environmental problem or something that was limited to a single group of Angels.

She didn't know the numbers off the top of her head but there were millions upon millions of Angels spread out all across the Empire and beyond. All of them were exposed to different environments, different levels of radiation and different factors that probably caused genetic instability.

Yet this was affecting everyone so it had to be present in the Angel DNA from the very start. And whatever this change was it had to somehow develop or manifest over 90,000 years later.

That was fascinating and Catherine couldn't wait to find out what the fault was.

***

Catherine ran her fingers across the icy cold white plastic of her holographic slab as she entered her ancient lab. Hundreds of different biologists, geneticists and other lesser scientists had dared to work here since she was last here. But she didn't mind, there were so many bright, amazing minds in the Empire that she was happy that they were still making discoveries after she had left.

The lab might have been tens of kilometres below the Empire Palace but Catherine loved how naturally cool and refreshing it was. The immense rocky cave walls of the lab were rough, textured and filled with holo-images of various tests currently going on.

She was really impressed with some of the research going on, but considering there was a massive naked superhuman corpse on her slab, she was a little more interested in that.

Catherine liked it when a small holographic lab assistant appeared next to her to make notes, and Catherine had no intention of using her so she simply clicked her fingers. The hologram went away.

The superhuman corpse was certainly female in perfect health besides the rotting flesh, bullet holes in the chest and brain matter that was currently leaking into a bucket on the floor. Catherine was going to have to test that matter later on, but the Angel was clearly deranged when she was killed.

The entire lab smelt refreshing of damp, mint and strawberries. It was one of her favourite smells, the Emperor had clearly remembered how she liked to work. He really was a great man.

Catherine picked up a scalpel from the small metal table next to her to and sliced open the superhuman's chest. The organs were awful, deformed and everything was wrong.

"I need to know the background of this Angel," Catherine said.

"Of course," the Ignis Angel said. "This is Officer Emma Young of the Knifer Legion. Many, many victories on the field of battle, she's killed over two thousand aliens, ten thousand traitors and she singlehandedly injured the Sabretooth,"

Catherine nodded. The Sabretooth was a massive and powerful and deadly leader in the Galaxy Burner traitor legion. As far as Catherine knew no one who had faced him had ever lived to tell the tale.

Emma was clearly a skilled, gifted and amazing warrior. That only made this entire situation even more tragic.

"A month ago she attacked her forces and went rogue. She killed two hundred soldiers in the Empire Army before her best friend killed her with three shots to the chest. Then she was sent back to Earth for examination,"

Catherine collected a blood sample and a small robotic arm dropped down from the ceiling, she passed the arm the sample and the arm immediately started testing it.

"Has anyone worked on this project?" Catherine asked.

"Negative, the Emperor believed since you are the Mother of Angels only you should work on this case,"

Catherine smiled. She really had missed Earth, the Emperor and the Empire Palace. She was actually surprised how much she felt at home here and how badly she had missed everything.

"Even if the DNA sample does come back corrupted," Catherine said, "even my memory isn't good enough to remember what all 23 chromosomes of an Angel should look like. I need an uncorrupted DNA sample,"

Catherine looked at the Angel and he was frowning.

"All Angel Genetic samples are corrupted too," he said, "but there is one sample we have,"

Catherine went over to him. She could tell how pained, concerned and puzzled he was. There was something he wasn't telling her and she made sure she had the scalpel firmly in her hand just in case.

When she had countered traitor Angels before, she had learnt that the Angels really did see her as their mother and they refused to hurt her. But even the damn traitors could be reasoned with, if the genetic instability was causing massive problems then she didn't want to take any chances.

"I can feel this rage inside me," the man said. "I have to get that sample for you,"

Catherine watched as the Angel went off to get the sample for her, but she secretly activated a small hologram that scanned the Angel. He wasn't wrong, his DNA had already degraded by 50% so she knew she was about to have a massive problem on her hands.

At least the Angel didn't have a gun. Not that having a gun was the only way an Angel could kill, Catherine had designed them to rip their enemies limb from limb and now she realised that might have been a mistake.

A beep echoed in the lab.

Catherine read the results of the DNA sample taken from the corpse and then she ordered the brain matter in the bucket to be tested.

She was impressed as hell about the sheer extent of the genetic instability. She was expecting maybe two or three of the chromosomes to be annihilated but all of them were being damaged beyond repair then Catherine ran another test.

She wanted to see when did the degradation start.

It started two years ago, and that confused Catherine. The degradation had to start in all the Angels had the same time, like it had been activated by something or someone and then she supposed that because of the various environments, different Angels went into some of the degradation happened faster.

Then for other Angels it took a little more time. It was fascinating and Catherine really did love her job.

"Doctor!" the Angel shouted.

The shout was deafening and Catherine covered her ears but she noticed that her ears were already deaf. Hopefully it was just temporary.

Catherine tried to scream but she didn't know if sound came out.

The Angel charged at her.

Catherine ducked to one side.

The Angel grabbed her by the throat.

Slamming her down onto the floor.

All the air rushed out of her lungs.

The Angel whipped out a knife.

Slamming it into her stomach.

Catherine swung the scalpel.

Ramming it into his throat.

Dark red rich blood poured out.

Catherine pushed it in further.

The Angel grinned as he ripped out the blade.

Thrusting it back into her stomach.

Catherine ripped out the scalpel.

Slamming it into the Angel's eye and into its brain.

The Angel's corpse collapsed to the ground and Catherine smiled because she was the master of genetics and she had designed the Angels to her ideals, values and promises of creating a better humanity.

It was a little-known trick but Catherine scooped up some of the Angel blood in her hands and pulled it into her wounds. She had given the Angels an extremely fast and effective way to heal themselves so it was even harder for them to die.

And thankfully the same blood and genetics that allowed them to heal faster could be used on normal humans too.

Catherine bit back the pain as her body healed itself and then she went over to the other side of the lab where she noticed the Angel had bought her the DNA sample before he had turned completely.

She went back over to the corpse, handed it to the robot arm and ran the test. At least the brain matter test was back and it only confirmed the sheer extent of the genetic corruption but it revealed something else too.

Someone had activated the genetic corruption.

Catherine flat out couldn't understand what the hell had happened. She had always been so damn careful about her work, her experiments and everything the Angels did. The only other people that could have accessed her research freely without her knowing (even that was an impossible mission) were the Emperor and the Lord Commander Garrison but he had been dead for 90,000 years.

Then Catherine realised there was one other person who could have been evil, manipulative and skilful enough to pull off everything.

Sarah Oddballa.

That crazy, twisted woman that Catherine really didn't

understand. It wasn't known if Sarah was for or against the Empire, no one understood her end goals and no one understood her aims and methods.

Catherine had tried to keep an eye on her old friend over the thousands of years but it was useless. Sarah was a mad ghost that went world to world, did something and then fled.

It was impossible to track her but the sheer intelligence this sort of predetermined genetic corruption required had her name written all over it.

Catherine smiled as she finally figured out what had happened and as the uncorrupted DNA sample returned with great results, Catherine had an idea about how to fix all of this and make sure that Sarah Oddballa's work was denied forever.

Catherine had her creations to save, an Empire to save and most importantly she had to protect the Emperor she seriously loved.

***

After two long days of testing, experimenting and doing such complex genetic work that even Catherine's head was starting to hurt, she had finally done it. She had finally come up with a way that could easily, cheaply and effectively repair the genetics of every single Angel in the Empire.

She had no doubt that the traitors would learn of her Gene Therapy and they would attack some supply ships looking for the cure themselves, and she was sort of okay with that. All of the Angels were her creations, her children and her babies so she supposed they all deserved a chance at life no matter who they served.

As Catherine stood on the very edge of the massive circular platform again and she enjoyed the sweet aromas of mint, watermelon and coconut, she knew that she was really going to miss Earth. She might even miss the tens upon tens of long lines of blade-like shuttles, warships and cruisers that created a traffic nightmare.

That was doubtful.

She had spoken to the Emperor, that God of a man, and she was more than happy to know how much he loved her, and she loved him.

Of course a relationship could never happen but by God did she wish it could at times. The Emperor was just an amazing, wonderful man but his focus had to be on defending humanity and ensuring that humanity survived no matter the cost.

Catherine understood that and it was why she was leaving again. There was an entire galaxy to explore beyond Earth. There were so many secrets to uncover, genetics to experiment with and even more biological samples to collect.

Maybe the key to humanity's survival was out there in the stars and if she could help humanity survive for at least another day, week or year then Catherine was going to take that chance and go exploring. Regardless of how dangerous the path ahead seemed.

She had to do it for herself, her Empire and definitely for her Emperor.

AUTHOR OF AGENTS OF THE EMPEROR
CONNOR
WHITELEY
GAMING FOR
A SYSTEM
A SCIENCE FICTION SPACE OPERA SHORT STORY

GAMING FOR A SYSTEM

Of all the ways of The Great Human Empire had fought wars, killed their enemies and defended humanity, Commander Harrison Thomas had to admit that playing a game with the winner taking over an entire solar system had to be the flat out weirdest way that he had ever heard of. Yet that was exactly what he was doing now.

Harrison stood in a massive spherical chamber with beautiful thick smooth blue walls made from the finest marble in the galaxy, little lines of blue light pulsed up and down the walls giving the chamber such warmth and there was a very large hovering metal platform that Harrison stood on now.

He had to admit the metal platform was strange and he actually felt a little sick whenever he looked over the edge, staring down at the bottom of the spherical chamber tens of metres below him. He didn't know who had created the chamber, all he knew was that this was where he had to play a game with the leader of the traitor forces to determine the fate of a solar system.

Harrison really wasn't a fan of the icy coldness of the chamber that chilled his skin, despite him wearing thick black body armour that hummed ever so slightly as the armour tried to keep his body warm. Harrison was really starting to wonder if the armour was going to work, or if he was actually going to freeze in here.

That's exactly how cold it was.

As another pulse of blue light went up and down the chamber's smooth walls, Harrison noticed that at the very top of the spherical chamber, there was a little orb-like device. The orb was as black as night, and the longer Harrison looked at it the more he felt a little unsure of himself, like the device was feeding into all his self-doubt about his abilities as a commander, friend and father.

Besides the gentle humming of his armour as it tried (and failed) to keep him warm, there wasn't any sound in the chamber. That alone was flat out disturbing to Harrison considering he was one of the unfortunate souls that had been born on the blade-like warships of the Empire.

He had always known sound. The first thing he had heard all those years ago wasn't the laughter or talking or smiling of his mother and father, it had been the gentle hum of the bright piston-like engines as they pushed the blade-like warship through the cold void of space.

Harrison had always known sound and whenever he didn't hear the almost silent background noise of the engines, he always struggled to focus because it was such a big sound that was missing from his life and his environment.

But the weirdest thing about the spherical chamber just had to be the strange smell of freshly smoked salmon, cod and rotten mackerel, and even worst Harrison really, really hated the foul taste of greasy fried fish on his tongue. The fish smell was so overwhelming that Harrison seriously wanted to pass out.

At least that way he wouldn't have to put up with that awful smell that defined all logic, considering he was literally the only other thing in the chamber, and he sure as hell didn't smell of rotten fish.

"Player Two Joining Soon," a loud computerised voice said.

Harrison wanted to take a few more steps closer to the relatively small centre of the metal platform he was standing on, but he was almost too scared to move.

He just knew that the metal platform was perfectly safe but because it truly looked and felt like it was just hovering there, he stupidly believed that too much movement actually would cause it to fall or tilt.

Harrison just smiled at himself because he really was being silly, and he really blamed the Empire Army for keeping him so trapped in the silver oval bridge of his destroyer class blade-like warship, instead of allowing him to explore the galaxy like he wanted.

All Harrison had really wanted was a little more freedom to explore the Empire with, at least that way he would actually have an opportunity to see what the galaxy was like. Maybe that way he wouldn't be so scared of moving on a hovering metal platform.

A bang echoed around the spherical chamber and the pulses of blue light became more and more frequent.

Harrison just watched as on the other side of the metal platform two columns of blue smoke swirled, twirled and whirled round each other for a moment until a figure appeared and Harrison seriously wasn't happy with what he saw.

And now his mission was crystal clear.

Harrison just stared with utter horror as he focused on the three-metre-tall superhuman soldier wearing his crimson red battle armour that was styled on medieval knight armour from ancient Earth, and Harrison really focused on the massive gun attached to his waist.

The gun alone was probably the size of Harrison's chest.

Thankfully, the superhuman had his face helmeted, Harrison really didn't want to see what monstrous face called that superhuman body home.

Harrison couldn't believe that after all the intense fighting in both space, ground and the atmosphere of the planets that the superhuman traitors had decided to negotiate with Earth that the fate of the solar system they were all fighting over would be decided with a simple game.

Harrison wasn't even sure what the point of fighting over the Domino System (at least that's what he believed the system was called. All the fighting and battles made those sort of pointless details so trivial) in the first place.

The entire 8 planet system used to belong to some dumb alien race with two heads, four beetle-like arms and a snail-like tail but the

Empire had wiped them out and now the traitors wanted it for themselves.

Harrison was flat out against just giving over Empire territory to those monsters so he was going to fight and win this game no matter what.

"Game Mode Selection Starting," a computerized voice said.

A hissing sound filled the icy cold air as the superhuman unsealed his helmet and the pressurized air escaped, revealing a cold face filled with twisted tattoos, scars and shattered jawbones that Harrison just found utterly disgusting to look at.

"This is what you're Empire did to me," the superhuman said.

Harrison just shrugged. Harrison was hardly going to apologise or something, it was exactly what the superhuman deserved after daring to betray the glorious Emperor for stupid and pathetic reasons about the traitors wanting their own power, influence and evil justice.

"Why are we playing?" Harrison asked.

The superhuman face twisted into a strange type of grin. "Because you know what legion I am from and you know I want to have a little fun. Why would I kill so many fleshy juicy humans when I can simply win a game and get you to leave in peace?"

Harrison seriously wasn't impressed with this superhuman, and he was sadly right, out of the nine superhuman Legions that the Emperor created, 6 had turned traitor and Harrison just wasn't happy that he was facing a superhuman from the Hydra Legion.

A legion that specialised in disinformation and spying. Basically they were tricksters in plain sight.

Definitely not the sort of people Harrison wanted to be playing a game with.

"Game Selected," the computerised voice said. "Welcome to the First and Only Round of Domino Death,"

Of all the stupid games in the Empire, Harrison seriously hadn't wanted to play Domino Death. He had only heard of this so-called legendary game once or twice in his life and the result was always deadly.

From what he understood of the game, the two players would have to match numbers on silver dominos made from freshly killed human bones and whoever lost the game would die.

But what concerned Harrison even more than the whole dying thing was that he had also sadly heard that electric currents randomly went through each of the dominos, and if a person touched one of the electrified pieces then they would get a very nasty electric shock.

A shock that grew in intensity with each turn.

Harrison was seriously not looking forward to this.

"Traitor Superhuman Selected as Player One," the computerised voice said.

Harrison just frowned as a small wooden table materialised in front of him, Harrison wasn't a fan of its icy cold wooden tabletop that was perfectly smooth and covered in twenty silver dominos made from bone. They were all ranged in a perfect grid and they might have looked perfectly safe but Harrison just knew that that wasn't true in the slightest.

"You want to quit now?" the traitor superhuman asked, his voice booming and deafening.

Harrison shook his head, if he quit now then an entire solar system would be damned to being ruled by monstrous traitors and the dying rule of the game would still be in effect.

Only one of them was leaving this chamber alive.

The superhuman tapped one of his dominos and Harrison quickly realised that the superhuman could easily survive a lot more electric shocks than him.

A bright blue hologram appeared in the centre of the metal platform showing a large picture of the domino that the superhuman selected.

It was a simple piece that Harrison would have picked, it had six dots on both ends, limiting the options of the enemy player but still giving them just enough options to make the game last a little longer.

Harrison had even heard of Domino Death games lasting three turns before they were over and the losing player was dead. Harrison just seriously hoped this superhuman wasn't that skilful of a player.

Harrison looked down at his dominos perfectly arranged in a grid pattern and he touched a domino with six dots at one end and a single dot at the other end.

The superhuman laughed.

Harrison was just glad not to get an electric shock for now.

The Superhuman hesitated before playing and just looked at Harrison. "Do you really know what is going on here?"

Harrison shrugged. Of course he did, he was playing a game to save a solar system, his career and making sure the traitors were defeated.

"You clearly don't," the superhuman said. "This game is rigged against both of us. My legion created this chamber for us both to die in, as we speak my Legion is attacking a sleeping Empire army fleet as they believe we wouldn't attack until the game was over,"

Harrison's frown only grew. This was so typical of the traitors.

"You are one of the leading Commanders in the defence of the system so you need to die," the superhuman said. "And my legion wants me dead or me to prove myself because of my failures on past missions,"

Harrison smiled a little. He could hopefully work with that, a man that needed to prove himself could be manipulated and desperate.

The superhuman pressed a domino and Harrison swore under his breath as a hologram of a domino with six dots at both ends appeared.

Harrison looked down at his pieces and there weren't any more pieces with six dots on them, and he only had a single domino with another single dot on one end and it had five dots on the other end.

Harrison pressed it and hissed as a small electric shock flew up his arm.

The superhuman went again using a domino with a five dot piece and a single dot on the other end.

Harrison was screwed. He didn't have any more dominos to play and if he pressed an incorrect one then he would automatically lose the game and end and the traitors would be free to invade the entire solar system and rule it forever.

Harrison couldn't allow that.

The Superhuman smiled. "You lost already?"

Harrison didn't even speak. He couldn't, he wasn't sure if his voice would crack or something, he was feeling so much guilt, anger and disappointment at himself.

He should have known the traitors they would attack his fleet whilst he was playing some kind of stupid game but all games, even rigged ones, could be won in the end.

Harrison just wanted, needed to just find how the hell he was meant to fix all of this.

And he just knew it all came down to trying to outsmart the Hydra Legion. They were the ones that set up the rigged game in the first place and the amazing thing about Domino Death was that you could still kill your opponent without having to win the game itself.

All Harrison needed to do was make sure the superhuman touched an electrified domino but of course that wouldn't work as whatever piece Harrison touched next would kill him. All because he didn't have another correct domino that had a single dot on one end.

"I'll time call you," the superhuman said.

"No you won't because the rules of Domino Death says this is an illegal game," Harrison said, having absolutely no idea if this was true or not.

The superhuman cocked his head slightly. "Liar. Domino Death is not an Empire Sanctioned Game, it does not have its own Governing Organisation,"

Harrison loved it when the enemy helped him by giving him certain pieces of information. Now he only had to convince the superhuman that there was.

"I'm surprise," Harrison said standing up perfectly straight. "I thought the Hydra Legion knew everything but you are a failure in the eyes of your Legion so I still won't forgive you, but there is a governing organisation of Domino Death,"

The superhuman spat at Harrison. His acidic spit burning a small hole in Harrison's body armour.

"Liar," the superhuman said.

"This is why you're a failure in the eyes of your legion," Harrison said. "Two weeks ago the EDDA, Empire Domino Death Association got founded and rested official guidance on how to play the game. And according to their rules this is a sham game and an illegal one!"

The superhuman shook his head. "It doesn't matter. My Legion will burn your Empire to the ground. They will kill your friends, your family, your everything!"

"Superhuman had admitted lack of legality of the game," the computerised voice said.

"What!" the superhuman shouted.

Harrison took a few steps back as the blue light that pulsed up and down the smooth walls of the chamber got a lot faster.

The superhuman smashed his fist down on the wooden table with all his silver domino pieces.

"Player 1 has played a domino out of turn. He loses the game," the computerised voice said.

Harrison loved it how the superhuman's eyes lit up and widened in utter horror as the entire chamber hummed, popped and banged.

The superhuman just glared at Harrison. "You!"

The superhuman charged at Harrison.

But Harrison just knew that he didn't have to react or anything because he had won and he just had a little feeling that the spherical chamber was always going to protect its winner.

A massive lightning bolt shot down from the ceiling.

Turning the superhuman to ash.

Thick blue columns of smoke swirled, twirled and whirled around Harrison as he was teleported off to safety and he really had to finish off these traitors once and for all.

***

A day later, Harrison sat in his large bright white office with yellow orbs of light hovering just below the smooth blue ceiling, giving the office such a wonderful sense of spaciousness and Harrison really did love his office.

Harrison sat on his smooth metal desk chair that was perfectly warm against his bum and back and shoulders, he didn't feel any discomfort thankfully, and it really was the perfect place to sit on so he could use his silver metal desk that hovered in front of him.

Harrison had spent the past day fighting, giving orders and shouting at members of his command crew from his oval bridge about how to destroy the traitor forces that were attacking them, and thankfully after a full day of fighting them had managed to win the battle.

And the Hydra Legion were in full retreat.

On Harrison's desk, he had dealt himself some jet-black dominos and he was just playing by himself. He really liked the coldness of them against his touch, and the freshly opened pack made the air smell of damp and refreshing so the dominos were probably packed up on some jungle world somewhere in the Empire.

It was a very nice change to the strange fishy air of the spherical chamber.

But as Harrison moved the little pieces of dominos about as he played faster and faster against him, he was really surprised at the sheer power of games and what they meant to different people.

Games had the power to give people pleasure, they had the power to exchange solar systems from the hands of good guys to bad guys and vice versa, and most importantly games had the power to kill people. Harrison really didn't wish the latter on anyone else but that was war at the end of the day.

So as Harrison finished up playing dominos by himself, he was so glad to have the small almost-invisible humming of his blade-like warship's engines in the background and he just knew exactly what he was going to do moving forward.

He was always going to keep fighting the enemy, protecting

humanity and surprisingly enough, he was going to keep playing games by himself and his amazing crew. Because games were powerful and Harrison seriously wanted to be the most powerful player in the galaxy for the sake of the Emperor.

And he just knew that was going to be a hell of a lot of fun indeed.

AUTHOR OF AGENTS OF THE EMPEROR SERIES
CONNOR WHITELEY
FARMING RESTRICTION
A SCIENCE FICTION FAR FUTURE SHORT STORY

FARMING RESTRICTIONS

Farming Director Adam Grant leant against the wonderfully warm balcony made from soft, sweet marble that was freshly shipped in from some random colony that he didn't care about. The soft refreshing, slightly warm breath brushed his cheeks and he was so looking forward to today.

His balcony was attached to an immense circular spaceship painted black that hovered just off the hard, cracked ground of Ceres 14. A beautifully lush planet most of the time but right now, that statement was in question.

For as far as Adam could see the ground was yellow, hard and cracked and it made no sense at all considering it rained twice a week on this planet, just as the glorious Rex had designed it. The latest data suggested the dryness of the planet was spreading a little too quickly for Adam's liking and sooner or later it would be impossible to grow crops on.

It was also strange and a little confusing that the large mountains and rolling hills of the planet that had been filled with olive trees, vegetables and more only yesterday were now completely empty, and the hills were mostly flat.

He supposed there could have been some kind of environmental reason for it all, but Adam had been working here for two decades now and this had never happened before. The environmental systems that destroyed the planet's natural weather systems were in perfect working order so all of this should have been impossible.

Adam really enjoyed the large, fat sun beaming down on him sending gentle warmth through his body and the sweet smells of corn, strawberries and honey filling the air from the latest harvest.

Possibly the last harvest for a long while.

Adam hated to imagine what Earth and the Rex would say when news of their crisis reached them. All Adam had wanted was a nice position of watching fruit, vegetables and livestock grow and he might have to do some paperwork from time to time but clearly he was actually going to have to do something.

He flat out hated the idea of that. And he hated the implications of the dryness of the planet even more. Everyone in the Imperium knew that the Rex only delivered food and water to planets that showed the most devotion to him and their dedication to rewrite history in his image.

It was only a month ago when he had been ordered to deliver two warships filled the most nutritious vegetables to reward a mining colony for killing all their history professors and over two thousand rebels who hated the Rex's rule.

Adam didn't agree with rewarding murder and bloodshed in the slightest but the Rex was the ruler of the Imperium and until anyone had the balls to rise up against him. Nothing would ever change in the Imperium.

And things would only continue to get worse and worse. Adam hated it how he had already been ordered to *decrease* food production by 20% over the past year to "give the populous of the Imperium more incentive to worship the Rex".

Adam's hands formed fists at the very notion of him not being able to do his job and actually have to make innocent people starve because of the Rex's twisted ideology. It was bad enough that the Imperium only allowed food to be grown on Farming Worlds that were highly, highly regulated but it was just stupid to have every single thing Adam did watched and approved by Earth.

Earth was just stupid.

"Chief," a woman said behind him.

Adam forced himself not to jump as the woman's voice sliced through the relaxing silence of the warm morning, he had wanted to enjoy the peace for a few more moments but that was never going to happen with a crisis unfolding around him.

Especially when he turned to face the woman and he was surprised she was wearing the black battle armour of the Imperial Army. Her medals and stripes and crowns on her armour told Adam everything he needed to know.

He was in the presence of one of the Imperium's high-ranking military officers. She was a Lord Commander, probably the Lord Commander of this entire sector of space and that never ended well.

As she came over to Adam and leant next to him, he had to admit with her long beautiful eyelashes, perfect smile and smooth skin she was certainly beautiful. Even her jasmine-scented perfume was a luxury Adam could never afford so why was a very rich and well-to-do commander visiting his little slice of hell?

"I was sent by Earth directly to investigate the matter of your planet," the woman said. "I am Lord Commander Isabella Coze,"

Adam forced himself not to frown as she said her name. Everyone, even the people living under rocks, knew of Commander Coze and how she enjoyed watching entire planets, races and populations get burnt alive for the smallest of infractions against the Imperium.

If she was here then his fate was already sealed. Not including the fate of all his workers, crops and the billions of people that relied on his food production.

"The Rex proposes that you have broken many Farming Restrictions and this is His Will and Plan to make you suffer," Coze said.

Adam shook his head. He knew that the Rex believed himself to be some kind of deranged god but he wasn't. And it was flat out impossible that Rex and his so-called divine power could reach through hundreds of thousands of solar systems to Ceres just to make the planet dry.

And if Coze believed it then she was a dick.

"I do not believe him," Coze said. "I believe there is a real cause to this planet's problems and whilst I am under rules to command you to build churches to the Rex. I am more concerned about my own military's food supply,"

Adam made sure his face didn't react because even Coze just admitting the Rex was wrong was more than enough to earn her a very slow, painful and agonising death.

"Where did the problems start?" Coze asked.

Adam shook his head. "They didn't. Everything just happened in front of my worker's eyes working the night shift last night. All three affected areas of the planet were impacted at once,"

Adam hated saying it out loud because it was like some strange personal failing but Coze was here now and he couldn't fail her. Otherwise everything he had ever wanted, built and aspired to would be obliterated and erased from history like every single thing in the Imperium was being.

"I'll take you to the largest impacted area now," Adam said and he walked away before Coze could answer.

He just hoped beyond hope this exploration would get everyone he cared about killed.

***

Adam was seriously surprised how difficult it was to get to the largest impacted area, it might have been on the other side of the planet but for some reason all the workers refused to go there. It also seemed like the machines and shuttles and drones refused to travel there either.

Adam wasn't sure if that had more to do with the drones and other pieces of technology being programmed to only travel to fertile ground, but it was still strange.

After two hours of trying to find a shuttle to take them there, Adam and Coze stepped off the black metal ramp of the circular shuttle and stood on the hard, cracked orange ground.

As the circular shuttle zoomed off into the distance like it was a child running away from a monster, Adam couldn't believe it as he stared out into the distance that stretched on for hundreds of miles, he just couldn't see anything but hard cracked flat land.

This was actually one of the most hilly areas of the planet and that made it perfect for growing grapes, grazing sheep and cows and even creating some genetic hybrids that the Rex said were illegal. Coze didn't need to know that of course.

But now Adam just couldn't believe how an entire farming ecosystem that had been thriving for over twenty years had disappeared overnight and the impacted area was spreading.

The air smelt burnt, crispy and there was a strange undertone of charred flesh that made no sense too.

"What did your workers describe happened?" Coze asked.

Adam shrugged. "They reported working on a hill, picking grapes at night because it's cooler. Then the next moment they were on flat hard, cracked ground with no grapes in their baskets,"

Coze shook her head. "If this is a trick then I swear to you I will kill you,"

Adam shook a few steps away. "Why would I play a trick on you? I didn't even know I supplied the military with food,"

"You don't. At least not yet but the Rex is rearranging how the Imperium's food production works so your planet will become military-only food,"

Adam threw his arms up in the air. "What about all the billions of people that rely on my planet for food? We both know the Rex will not allow them to grow their own food and he will not offer them another Farming World as their source of food,"

Coze grinned. "At least I'm not the only traitor on this planet,"

Adam hardly believed himself to be a traitor to humanity just because he didn't agree with billions of people starving but maybe that was the key to solving this mystery.

Adam knelt down on the hot cracked ground and he was surprised how rough and almost razor sharp the ground was. None of this was natural and he had no idea who would have the technology to actually pull this off.

Except the Rex of course.

Adam looked at Coze. "Why is the Rex killing this planet?"

Coze shrugged. "Because… he isn't. He really isn't trying to kill you or the billions of planets that rely on you. He wants to kill me and my military planet,"

Adam smiled. He hadn't realised that the rumours were true, that the Imperial Army weren't stationed on normal planets and that they were actually stationed on their own planets. Probably some kind of military Fortress Planet.

"Why would he want to kill you?" Adam asked.

Coze looked up at the crystal clear sky for a moment before looking at Adam.

"Because I was wrong to follow the Rex and burn entire planets to the ground. The Rex is wrong and me and my planet have succeeded from the Imperium," she said.

Adam laughed. He had to admit that Lord Commander Coze was extremely ballsy and bold and stupid.

Everyone knew that no one just succeeded from the Imperium without their planet being turned into a wasteland.

"I control two billion soldiers and this entire sector of space," Coze said. "Me turning my back on the Imperium is a massive blow that the Imperium will quickly recover from so me and my forces are fleeing towards the Enlightened Republic,"

Adam laughed. "That's a myth. The Enlightened Republic is simply a myth designed by the Rex to give people false hope,"

Coze grabbed his wrist. "No. It isn't. I encountered a Republic cell operating on my planet and I interrogated them. They showed me proof and they showed me that there was a better way to live,"

Adam wasn't buying it. It was impossible to imagine that there was a group of humans able to live in peace without the constant oversight of the Rex.

"They're a group of solar systems on the furthest reaches of the Imperium that encourage people to learn, vote for democracy and live freely without the control of the Rex,"

Adam waved his hands about. "How does this relate to what's going on on my planet?"

Coze frowned. "The Rex must have learnt that I would come here first before setting off so we would have enough food to make the journey. And I didn't want to burden the Republic when we arrived so I wanted enough food for us to survive for maybe a decade,"

Adam nodded that seemed perfectly reasonable and it was an easy order to fulfil considering he normally sent enough food to last planets twenty or thirty years at a time.

Adam just shook his head as he watched a thin line of dust blew about in the wind and he found it hard to believe that two billion soldiers (a mere drop in the ocean of the Imperium's population and military might) was enough reason to justify destroying an entire Farming World that the Rex knew billions relied on for food.

That was murder to him and Adam had to admit that if the Enlighted Republic did exist then he certainly wanted to be apart of it.

He no longer wanted to live in an Imperium that had such discard for the lives of innocent humans that only wanted to feed themselves, their friends and most importantly their families.

***

Adam stood on an immense circular bridge of a bright white circular warship a few years later and he was just amazed as they entered the Enlightened Republic just how different it was.

They were thousands upon thousands of miles away from the border but the bright red, red and purple planets looked so magical and hopeful that Adam was so looking forward to the future.

He and Coze had become great friends over the past years, and Adam liked to think he had really helped her overcome her past and trauma about burning so many planets to ash. In all fairness she had hardly had a choice and she was only following her conditioning from the Rex.

He was that good at controlling people after all.

The bridge might have been empty with only the gentle hum of the engines keeping him company, but Adam liked how everyone in the fleet was enjoying their evening meals. And whilst he really hoped that the billions of people that relied on Ceres 14 had found another source of food, he still wasn't ashamed that as he, his staff and all of Coze's military lot emptied the planet of food to travel to the Enlightened Republic because it meant that they could help their new friends survive.

And Adam was no military man but he had a feeling that the Rex, his generals and spies were always watching, learning and studying the Enlightened Republic for the right moment to strike and claim it for themselves.

For any degree of peace, freedom or love in the galaxy was just a carefully crafted illusion by the Rex because he wanted humanity all to himself.

And he would never stop until all of humanity worshipped him and he controlled them all, but as long as Adam lived he was going to make sure that never ever happened and if making sure the Enlightened Republic had enough food was a way to do that, then he was perfectly happy with that.

AUTHOR OF AGENTS OF THE EMPEROR
CONNOR WHITELEY
MONSTER MAN
DIDN'T CREATE
A SCIENCE FICTION SOLARPUNK SHORT STORY

MONSTER MAN DIDN'T CREATE

I, David Victor, absolutely knew that humanity wasn't the perfect species in the past. We were killers, brutal and sometimes just flat out monsters as we could so easily enslave each other. And before the glorious Emperor united us, we would happily slaughter entire civilisations for the mere fun of it.

But thankfully we had changed.

Well, after this particular incident, that's a maybe. Now being a scientist, farmer and very sexy lover, I deal in very hard facts. I know how to grow certain crops, I could literally talk you to death about plant biology and I know that I'm an extremely good lover, well that's according to my boyfriend but I don't doubt him.

This case leaves me questioning a lot but I suppose I really should start at the beginning, please forgive me for not doing that in the first place. This case… was just a little chaotic and even now I'm a little rattled.

You see I am not just any scientist in the Great Human Empire, I'm a scientist that works on Holy Earth itself. Sadly not in one of its many fine universities, medical centres or research centres that can make people famous throughout the entire Empire. But I work in a single skyscraper that I fully believe transformed humankind for the better.

Since I was currently leaning against the perfectly warm glass railing on my glass balcony at the very top of my skyscraper, that was nicknamed the glass dagger by workers because it was an immense structure made completely of ecologically friendly glass with microscopic solar panels embedded into the glass fibres so the entire skyscraper in the shape of a dagger rising out of the ground was 100% self-efficient.

I loved leaning against my glass railings in the morning because I really loved staring down at all the immense floors below me since there was a hole in the middle of each floor that allowed me to look tens of kilometres below to the very bottom of the skyscraper.

And thanks to my amazing boyfriend, Pedro, buying me a single cybernetic eye last Emperor's Day, I had the enhanced vision to actually see the bottom.

Each floor was an amazing feat of engineering if I do say so myself because it's easily the size of some Old Earth cities like a strange place called London or New York, at least I think those were real places, the historical records are vague on those savage cities.

Anyway, each floor is like an immense canvas for me to decide what the hell I want to grow, develop and create on.

For example, the floor directly below me was an entire floor dedicated to growing wheat. I seriously love walking through the endlessly yellow wheat fields that feel so soft against my bare legs and feet as the wheat gently blows in an artificial wind.

It is a very beautiful sight that I do treasure.

Then about halfway down the skyscraper, there's a meat lab, where me and my scientists literally grow 100% tasty, rich and juicy meat out of molecules. All without the environmental damage that the real cows do and this method is definitely a lot less smelly. Exactly how I like it.

But I definitely save the best level for all the visitors and officials that pop in to inspect my building and the workers when they first come in in the morning. Because the ground floor of the building is dedicated to sea creatures.

Most mornings my amazing workers can see dolphins, humpback whales and prawns popping out of the water to welcome them into the building. I did say this place was massive mind you.

And a lot of inspectors have said that seriously makes a delightful first impression.

Exactly what I want to hear.

Yet I would say the only floor of the building that is remotely "normal" is my floor, the very top floor of the entire building. I turned around and just smiled as my perfectly plain glass floor filled with offices, hovering grey desks and green holographic computers that numbers of workers were working at.

But I have to admit my sexy boyfriend was definitely looking a lot more worried than he normally did.

Pedro had to be the most beautiful man I had ever met all those hundreds of years ago, and thanks to the advance rejuvenation treatments we buy each other we don't look a day over thirty, with his smooth sexy brown skin, gorgeous dark golden eyes and his strong manly jawline that made him look like a god in human form.

And he really was my god.

But as he sat at his hovering grey desk in his own corner office filled with holographic artwork, real clay vase and some more things I could only lovingly describe as utter shit, he looked to be having a very heated argument with someone on his holographic computer.

Now as his boyfriend and his boss, I was naturally conflicted. Because it was clearly work related judging by the pulsing vein out of his neck and he was clearly annoyed, meaning if I did go in then he was going to moan at me.

As a boyfriend I could live with that, as a boss I couldn't really.

For a moment I focused through Pedro's office window on a bright blue blade-like space shuttle that was slowly zooming off into the distance but then Pedro ended the call.

And he just folded his arms and I knew it was bad.

As much as I knew not to do it I went over to his office and I didn't even knock and I didn't stop until I was a metre from him.

He just glared at me, probably trying to decide if he should complain to me, or talk to me as a boyfriend or boss or even both. We had come up with some of our best bedroom games when we had combined the two roles, but I sadly realised now wasn't the time.

"What's wrong?" I asked, knowing someone had to break the silence between us.

Pedro glared at me and I felt like he was burrowing into my soul. "The Head of Security called me. We have a body found in the wheat fields,"

My mouth dropped. What the hell? How the hell did that happen? More importantly who the hell died?

Pedro stood up and went over to the window. "That was my reaction at first but we have larger problems,"

Now I realise how bad that sounded, and I had to catch myself when I started judging Pedro for believing there could actually be larger problems than having a dead body in the building, but then I realised that some of his other jobs for me was media management, making sure the Empire didn't shut us down and making sure our trade routes stayed open.

I didn't like a single one of those things changing.

"Someone has already alerted the Arbiters and they already have someone on-site," Pedro said.

"Shit," I said.

Now just in case you are an Empire supporter, please know I actually don't have anything against the Arbiters per se or anything about them. The Arbiters are great people, able to investigate crimes, convict and kill a criminal on site if needed, so they are basically laws onto themselves.

But to actually have someone like that in your building, poking their nose around your staff and crops. That is very scary, dangerous and that Arbiter could kill me very easily.

But worst, kill the beautiful man I love even quicker.

"Has the Arbiter found anything yet?" I asked.

Pedro smiled. "No, but babe, I sort of need to tell you something,"

I folded my arms. This so wasn't the time to find out my boyfriend had been keeping something from me.

"It was sort of me who called them and I didn't exactly call them only. I also called a very old friend because of the body,"

I really folded my arms and focused on Pedro's holographic computer that I was now only realising had the images of the dead body on.

I had no idea if it was a man or woman or alien at this point because someone or something had seriously slashed up the victim.

In fact judging by these images I doubt a person had done this at all. Those slash marks were way too deep.

"You didn't call Matty Laura did you?" I asked.

"I love you?" Pedro said but it sounded like a question.

Matty Laura wasn't exactly a man I liked, trusted or even respected very much because he was an Inquisitor. A member of the top-secret organisation of the Inquisition that acted as the Empire's most secret and powerful policing force. A single Inquisitor had the power to burn entire sectors, kill billions of people and do whatever the fuck they wanted.

So the fact that my beautiful boyfriend had called him and actually had the bullocks to do it, meant one of two things.

One, my boyfriend was very stupid and we definitely weren't going to have sex for quite a while.

Two, my boyfriend was extremely clever and he recognised we were dealing with something so dangerous and deadly and horrific that only an Inquisitor could help us.

Whatever it was I just knew we were in deep deep shit and I had absolutely no idea how to get us out of it.

***

The moment I went into the wheat fields floor, that was an amazing sight of endless kilometres of tall beautiful wheat blowing in the artificially warm wind with a bright artificial orange sun in the ceiling, I just knew that something was awfully wrong besides from the dead body that is.

I continued to walk through the wheat field, and I seriously savoured the wonderful feeling of the wheat brushing my trousers, tickling my hand as I reached out and brushed my fingers over the top of the crops, and I really enjoyed the soft warm breeze on my cheeks. That was something people on Earth didn't get to fill anymore.

I was so lucky.

But something had to be dangerously wrong because everything was slightly out. The bright orange of the wheat fields was wrong because at this time of the day it should have been more of a sunset colour, not bright and fiery. Even the air smelt wrong with hints of burnt ozone, fertilizer and the metal tang of vapourised blood forming on my tongue.

That shouldn't have happened at all.

After a few more moments of walking through the beautiful wheat fields, I heard Pedro run up behind me and then slow to a walk when we both noticed a very tall man in thick black body armour standing in the distance.

We went over to him knowing that he was Pedro's old friend Matty Laura, and an Inquisitor of the Emperor's Holy Inquisition.

I forced myself to go over to him as I felt my heart pound in my chest, my blood ran icy cold and my knees turned wobbly. And believe me, this was not an overaction to meeting an Inquisitor in the slightest.

When we went over to him as much as I wanted to focus on Matty, my eyes were immediately drawn to the disgusting corpse that laid at my feet.

The sheer smell of the corpse was overwhelming. I had never smelt a dead body before but it was so disgusting and I knew the smell would cling to me sadly.

"What do you see?" Matty asked.

I stayed silent as I focused on the ripped up shred corpse. The body had immensely deep and thick claw marks that slashed into the flesh.

All the internal organs seemed to have been devoured and the same went for the eyes, brain and tongue.

This wasn't exactly pleasant to look at and that was before I truly noticed all the blood that had leaked and sprayed and dripped everywhere.

"Whatever happened I doubt a baseline human did this," Pedro said deadly serious.

It took me a few moments to realise that my sexy boyfriend was saying that anyone short of the superhuman soldiers of the Empire called the Angels of Death and Hope could have done this. But that was equally impossible.

There was no reason for a superhuman to be inside my building.

"Negative," Matty said. "There is another explanation,"

I realised as I looked at Matty that this was the first time since I had come here that I had actually looked at Matty properly.

He was really hot in a way with his smooth caramel coloured skin, war-hardened face and beautifully bright eyes that told me exactly what I needed to know. This man had seen both the best and worst that the galaxy had to offer.

And judging by the thick body armour in a very well-fitting shape. I was very willing to bet he had an amazing body under that armour, and at least now I knew why my boyfriend had spoken so fondly of him over the years.

"What explanation?" I asked and Pedro stepped forward.

"What creatures and animals do you have in this facility?" Matty asked.

I shrugged. "Nothing that could have done this. I don't even think we have any creatures with claws,"

Matty smiled. "That is not what I asked. What I actually want to know is do you have any creatures from Galactic north?"

"Yes," Pedro said folding his arms. "We have a number of species from pollinators to ocean creatures to some kind of alien… bear,"

As soon as the words left Pedro's sexy lips I realised what had happened because that was the thing about humans and biologists and their damn experiments. We were always testing new genetics to see if we could create stronger crops.

But we also tested on animals and creatures to see if we could create better bees and more to help the whole growth process become more efficient and natural. What if a biologist had created the creature that had killed this person?

"I doubt any man made this," Matty said as I noticed the massive battery-operated shotgun hanging on his waist.

"Then what?" I asked.

Something rustled in the wheat fields.

"The problem with the North is that some of those creatures can adapt, breed and take on the characteristics of other creatures,"

"A Genetic Hybrider," Pedro said.

Shit.

This was extremely bad. I had only heard of these creatures a few times over the centuries but these creatures could suck the blood out of two different creatures that biologically couldn't mate and the Hybrider could happily combine them.

To effectively create monsters.

No one knew why the hell they did it and there were no real theories but right now I didn't care.

We had a Hybrider lose on Earth itself or hopefully only in this building and it had created a monster capable of slaughtering my staff.

The rustling got louder.

I activated my cybernetic eye and noticed something very warm running about in the wheat field.

I changed a setting to see it clearly.

My mouth dropped.

It was a massive bear-like creature easily the size of a cow from Old-Earth. It had metre-long claws, slashing teeth and it looked to be covered in a thick layer of metallic fur.

It charged at us.

I deactivated my eye and leapt to one side.

Throwing Pedro to the ground.

We both jumped up.

The Inquisitor whipped out his shotgun. He fired.

The pellets deflected off the bear.

Shooting into Matty. He hissed. He screamed.

The bear chomped down on his leg.

I charged over. Pedro followed me.

I didn't have a weapon. Only instinct.

I jumped into the air.

Kicking the bear.

It didn't move.

The bear roared.

It swung around.

Whacking me with its head.

Throwing me to the ground. It charged at me.

The bear opened its jaw.

Trying to bite my head off.

I gripped its jaws. Forcing them to stay open.

Pedro charged over.

Firing the shotgun.

The bear screamed.

Pedro threw the shotgun at me.

The bear jumped.

Catching the shotgun.

It chomped down.

The battery casing exploded.

The bear screamed.

I flew over.

Punching the bear in the eye.

Pedro did the same to the other.

The bear looked like it was recovering.

I had no choice.

I pressed my fingers into the bear's eyes.

It roared in agony.

Pedro pressed on the other eye.

The bear screamed in crippling pain.

Dark rich blue blood poured over my hand.

The bear collapsed to the ground. It was breathing.

Matty staggered over to the bear and using his reinforced-strength that his battle armour presumably provided him he stomped on the bear's head. Shattering it.

I just looked at my sexy boyfriend glad he was alive and Matty who was smiling at me like I had done something amazing.

And maybe I had but right now there were a lot more pressing issues to deal with. And finding the Hybrider and identifying the body and resecuring the building were all a little outside of my expertise.

"What to help out two friends again Inquisitor?" I asked.

Matty just laughed and now I knew I was going to see exactly how powerful Inquisitors were.

Something that both scared and delighted me in equal measure.

***

After the next few hours, I have to admit it was rather horrific to watch a mere fraction of the power held by a single Inquisitor, because the entire building went into lockdown, ten thousand Empire Army soldiers stormed the building and they searched every single inch of my domain searching for the missing Hybirder.

I was thankfully allowed to watch with Pedro on my green holographic computer screen and it was remarkable how brutal and powerful and scary the little Hybrider was when it was cornered. It was probably no larger than a monkey but its power was amazing.

It killed two hundred soldiers before it was put down and the corpse was taken away by the Inquisitor.

And as I stood in Pedro's large glass office with tasteless, awful holographic art on the glass walls, I just couldn't believe what had happened and the consequences of it all.

Before Matty had left and lifted the Inquisitorial orders on the building, he had told me in no uncertain terms that I was lucky to be alive and that Matty did not believe that I was responsible for bringing such a deadly creature to holy earth itself, but he believed someone was.

The air might have smelt perfectly pleasant of roses, lavender and Pedro's sexy aftershave as he was less than a metre from me, but I knew the entire building stunk of rot because I don't believe Matty was wrong. Matty must have known that Pedro would only love a man that was detailed, careful and almost paranoid about ever drawing the eye of the Arbiters, much less the Inquisition.

I truly believe that Matty knowing and trusting and probably loving Pedro at some point or another was what saved me today. Because the Inquisition rarely didn't burn entire buildings and people and families for a simple perceived infraction of the law.

But somehow a deadly Hybrider had made its way to Earth and if that creature had escaped the building then I would have hated to imagine how many people it would have killed, let alone what foul monsters it would have created.

I still seriously loved Pedro for notifying the dead man's wife earlier. He was always better at the emotional stuff than me, even in our amazing relationship he was the more expressive one and that was something I really loved about him.

But I still felt guilty in a way because the dead man was a nobody really. He was a farmhand that I had trained myself decades ago, we had laughed a few times but he was an innocent. He wasn't a target, a friend or anyone that was so critical to the building that it actually made sense to kill him.

He was a great worker and in all honesty everyone in this building is part of my family.

And I really do love them all.

Pedro wrapped his strong dark arms around me and kissed my neck slowly, he always was such a great boyfriend but he also had a point. This was no longer my concern, Matty had taken over the case and this was solely the Inquisition's problem now.

So I might have been a little (a lot) shaken by the whole murder, attack and nightmare of it all but that was all in the past. I had a building to run, crops to grow and a boyfriend to treasure. And none of those things were going to be hard or work in the slightest.

They were all going to be extremely fun and that was why I loved my life, and I really was living my best life imaginable.

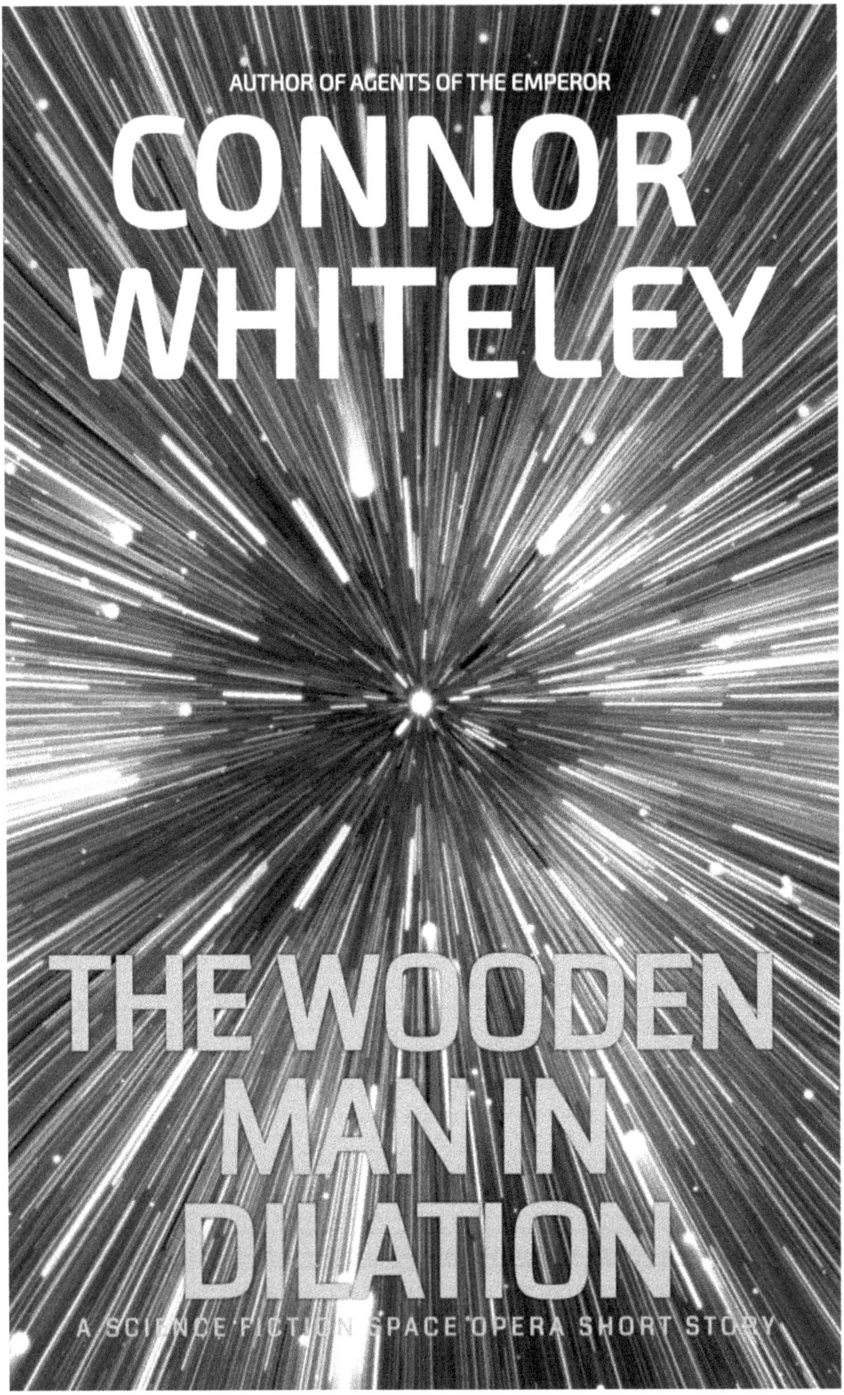
AUTHOR OF AGENTS OF THE EMPEROR
CONNOR WHITELEY
THE WOODEN MAN IN DILATION
A SCIENCE FICTION SPACE OPERA SHORT STORY

THE WOODEN MAN IN DILATION

I have absolutely no idea why humanity decided to try and build a machine that converted living flesh into wood, but hey, if I know anything about humans it is how… persistent they are in pushing their knowledge into some pretty extreme realms.

And now I was going to die today (or tomorrow or just some time very, very soon) because of it.

Well I suppose that I can't moan too much because I was one of those nutters, but unlike my nutter friends, I was stupid enough to ignore the sign outside the lab which said very clearly do not take off your safety glasses for any reason.

I was very, very stupid and I did.

Now I am completely made from wood. I have long smooth wooden arms, wooden legs and a wooden chest. I actually don't mind those things so much because I can still hear, see and taste things.

But I absolutely hate my face. You know I use to be called one of the hottest male scientists in the galaxy. Women loved my long brown hair, my striking blue eyes and my killer smile. Well now women just ran away from me.

And as I sit in my cold metal cockpit on a metal chair that no one should ever have to suffer through with nothing but an oval dashboard filled with switches, buttons and computer screens, I really don't like how everything turned out.

Granted there are a few advantages, I get to spend my days sitting watching the stars, planets and other space phenomena flash past my little squid-like ship on my little computer screens as they constantly scan my surroundings.

I've actually seen some pretty cool stuff like inhabitable planets, a wick nebula and plenty of other things that my old nutter friends would have loved to see.

And the amazing smell of lemony tea, poorly recycled air and cinnamon constantly filtered through the cockpit giving off the strangest, but nicest, of smells. Reminding me of delicious cinnamon rolls with lemon icing like my mother use to make when I was a wee boy.

Because of how disgusting I looked with all my wooden knots, nobs and cracks, the Earth Government thought I would be perfect for space missions to transport supplies to our far, far away colonies that would take human-manned ships centuries to travel to.

Of course most of those humans on the ships would age so much during that time that they would be, I quote, *'old and fat and useless by the time they completed the journey'*.

But hey, let's send out a wooden man instead because no one cares about him.

Fuck them is all I want to say!

The sound of my cockpit slowly popping, humming and vibrating made me sit up a bit more in my awfully cold and uncomfortable metal chair, I quickly checked the readings to see if the ship was experiencing any problems.

I've probably been on this ship now for a good seventy years and when I'm not playing some quiet music in the background, the ship's own sounds are barely audible.

In fact until now, I don't think I ever really knew what the ship sounded like, but the humming, popping and vibrating of the ship was getting louder and louder and louder.

I swiped away at my computer screen for a few more moments and I just had a feeling that I needed to check my speed, since my nutter friends told me once that these transport ships always become louder before they slowed down to dock at a planet.

Shoot! Shit! Fuck!

Of everything that could have gone wrong with my little squid ship, as I liked to call it, I seriously hadn't wanted the engines to slow down, and now my computer screens weren't responding to my touch. I couldn't even find out where I was, what speed I was going and how close I was to my final destination.

I was lost.

I was actually lost in space with no one knowing where I was and my biggest concern was I was easily twenty years away from the nearest habitable planet with any space fleet big enough to come and search for me.

Now if I was a normal fleshy human then I would probably be concerned about food, water and all that stuff (granted I could probably just look at my cargo and find those things), but as a wooden man I had a much, much bigger problem.

If I didn't get any wood polish, varnish or whatever crap you use to treat wood, I was going to start splintering very, very soon. So much so that I might start falling apart and there was even the risk of my wood being infected.

My long hard wood might be no more!

Now that was truly a problem.

A problem I needed to solve yesterday.

Because time was running out fast.

***

"*Dilation's Past* has disappeared my Lord,"

Of all the things Lord Commander Camila Bell had not wanted to hear this morning (or was it night? She had been working so hard lately) she seriously did not want to hear about the *Dilation's Past* going missing.

Camila just folded her arms as she stood in the massive oval bridge of her circular space station. She had never liked how cold the bare metal walls made the bridge but given how everyone here in rows were just hunched over their holographic computers relaying communications, giving orders and monitoring ship movements. She supposed it could have been worse.

Camila just had to find that ship. Especially because that sexy wooden man had been on the ship. Camila just couldn't help but smile to herself, she had really loved running her hands all over that hard sexy wood and him making her laugh like she was the most important woman in the galaxy.

Hints of bitter burnt coffee, harsh cleaning chemicals and pine-scented recycled air filled the bridge and Camila just wasn't sure what to do.

The *Dilation's Past* was almost like a cruel joke amongst humanity, the whole idea of it was that the ship would have such advanced engines that time dilation would basically be a thing of the past if it kept to its extreme speeds. But clearly that was never going to happen.

And now a poor innocent man was drifting in space because others deemed him too non-human to have around.

"Last reported location?" Camila asked.

A very short man stood up and bought Camila over a holographic tablet that showed everything they knew about the *Dilation's Past.*

"Unknown Lord," the man said. "We were monitoring the ship as it made its seventieth year on its trip then its transponder beacon just failed,"

Camila hissed as she felt her stomach knot at the realisation that her sexy wooden man had been gone for so long. Their wooden and fleshy bodies together only felt like yesterday.

"Have you tried scanning for the ship?" Camila asked.

The man looked as if he was going to laugh. "You do know how vast that sector of space is? He was basically travelling through a dead zone for our scanners, we only managed to track him as far as we did because of his beacon,"

"And that's gone we have no way of tracking him," Camila said.

The man nodded. "Should I order a fleet to start searching the area?"

As much as Camila wanted to shout yes and how badly she wanted to send every single available fleet to find the wooden man she probably loved. Camila just knew that she couldn't, not only would it be a waste of resources, but she could lose her job.

The Earth Government had wanted to get rid of the wooden man so badly, they would never accept one lonely woman (that wasn't really liked in the first place) wanting to find the man they wanted to die out in the cold void.

Camila just shook her head slowly. She really didn't want to give the order but she just had to.

"No," she said, "no fleets will be sent out. Contact Earth Command and see about a replacement ship for those supplies,"

The little short man bowed and quickly went off to his holographic computer.

As Camila stared out through the massive floor-to-ceiling windows of the oval bridge and back out into the stunning stars, she just hoped that in a few decades if any new technology was developed to help her find her wooden man. She just hoped he was still alive.

Camila really loved him.

And all she wanted to do was save the wooden man she really loved.

***

I think it took about two hours for me to realise that I was going to die here. I was out in the middle of space, no one knew where I was and I was just travelling through space at an unknown speed in an unknown direction.

Yep I was going to die.

But if I was going to die then I was going to make sure I died living the sort of life that I had always wanted. And that was where the absolutely amazing cargo and supplies I was carrying came in.

I went into the immense cargo storage area that was easily the size of a large city and I went straight over to the Lab section which sounded really fancy and everything, but it was nothing more than three incubators that were big enough for a normal human to stand up in for the colonists to grow some animals for themselves.

Because I'll tell you that I have wanted to be a farmer. I just think there's something so cool about growing your own food, harvesting it and just having fun. And it seriously beats the dehydrated crap that I was given for this mission.

So I went back over to the cargo, grabbed some of the chicken eggs, frozen goat embryos and some cow embryos, because every farm needs a cow, right?

I carefully placed them in the incubators and turned them on. Thankfully these incubators were cutting edge back in the day so my animals should be ready in about three days.

This was going to be amazing fun!

***

The *Dilation's Past* had been missing for twenty years now and Camila just felt terrible. Her joints ached, her body had been broken by more wars than she wanted to count and all her children had moved to systems far, far away.

As Camila sat on her warm rocking chair that overlooked the massive city of London with all its glass, high-tech buildings that rose up into the sky like daggers. Camila just pulled her blanket over herself tightly, she wasn't cold, she was just old.

The war with the different alien races of the galaxy had been so brutal, cold and calculated that Camila really didn't want to be Lord Commander anymore.

The things she had done in the name of victory, to protect humanity and just save herself had been… horrific.

And for what?

Camila had lost her husband of ten years to those alien bastards because she gave him accidental false information and now her kids hated her for killing their father. She didn't really blame them, sometimes Camila actually felt like she misled her husband on purpose, because he was nothing like that sexy wooden man from ninety years ago.

That tall sexy man with all those hard wooden muscles, killer smile and just… a loving personality. She really did love him because he was the only man who ever even tried to make her feel special.

And that was what she loved about him.

Camila felt her joints, bones and muscles start to ache and Camila really didn't know how much longer she had left to live.

But she just had to make sure she lived a little longer so she could find the *Dilation's Past* and hopefully see her beautiful sexy wooden man again.

***

Three days later I was just flat out amazed. I actually had five chickens, two goats and a cow! A real black and white cow that mooed and wow, just wow!

As I stared at them in the incubators I quickly realised that I didn't know what to do with them anymore. Of course I would have to feed them, care for them and love them. But then what?

Did I have to eat them, ride them or do something else?

It wasn't like I was going to live for too much longer anyway so I supposed I just had to make the most of this amazing farming life whilst I still could.

I went to move back over to the cargo and supplies to get some more animals when I just had to stop. My wooden arms and legs and chest were definitely not smooth anymore.

All the wood I was made of was beginning to crack a little, chip and I was starting to fall apart. I already had to cut off my own toes a day ago because they were starting to rot.

So it was only a matter of time really until the rest of me went to the massive bonfire in the sky, I just looked at my farm animals as I focused on that fact.

Then I realised how the animals had managed to open the incubators and they were out. A little chicken came over to me and started to peck my foot.

Ouch!

I might have been wood but I could still feel things. Wow, chickens can really hurt if they attack you.

But that was the amazing thing about all of this, so I went back over to the cargo and supplies to see what else I could create. There were so many wonderful choices here, there was literally every single type of animal here.

So I grabbed a couple more cows, some pigs and my personal favourite horses. You can never ever go wrong with horses, and whilst I wasn't stupid enough to ride them it sure would be fun to have them.

I quickly popped them back in the incubator and left them to grow for the next three days.

But as I noticed some of my rough wooden arms start to crumble away I just doubted I would last these final days.

If that was the case I was going to make my final days the best I possibly could!

***

Camila absolutely hated how the *Dilation's Past* had been missing for over fifty years now, Camila just knew that she was never going to see her beautiful sexy wooden man again.

And Camila was okay with that in a strange way, she had loved him more than she ever really wanted to admit. Yet even if he was still alive he probably wouldn't have given her a second look anyway.

Camila rested on the thin cold sheets of her hospital bed and just stared out through the floor-to-ceiling window that she had requested. Camila loved being in a hospital in high orbit of Earth, it was so beautiful, peaceful and like the entire world was at peace.

The sounds of Camila's life signs beeping on all on the hospital equipment around her made Camila really hate her life at the moment, she was dying and all the nurses and doctors and everyone else who cared to give an opinion said she only had a few hours left.

Everyone had said how great Camila had been at lasting this long with her bone cancer but she didn't feel it. All she had wanted for the past few decades was only one more chance to see her wooden man.

Camila had even managed to surprise herself in her determination, that sole focus had driven her on for years, and thankfully managed to stop her bone cancer for a little while.

But the cancer was fighting her more than ever, and each breath felt like it was taking more and more effort than it was actually worth. And Camila just knew she was never seeing her wooden man again.

Camila was losing hope and her very grown-up children, the nurses and the doctors no longer cared about her hope. Camila fully believed they all just wanted her to die so the hospital could have a spare bed and her children could get her wealth.

"Mum?"

Camila forced herself away from the amazing view of Earth from high-orbit and smiled when she saw a tall elegant woman walk in wearing a light blouse, white high-heels and some stunning white jeans.

Camila hadn't actually seen her middle daughter Kinsley for thirty years but she was so glad to see her now in her final hours.

"Kinsley," Camila said, as she started coughing.

Kinsley came over and took her mother's hands, Camila loved the feeling of human contact with her kids after so, so long.

"It's good to see you mum, and I found it for you," Kinsley said.

Camila shrugged. She had no clue what Kinsley could have found.

"I found the *Dilation's Past* for you,"

Camila held her daughter's hand tight as she realised what she was saying.

"I invented a new scanner for the Navy and we tested it on the region of space where the ship went missing. Of course we corrected for time and rough speeds it was traveling at, but we found it,"

Camila managed to force her body to kiss Kinsley's hands and realised she was getting weaker and weaker by the second. Camila looked at the door to her room just in case her sexy wooden man was going to walk in.

"There was only a week past on the ship but I'm sorry mum. He's dead," Kinsley said.

Camila hissed. "How?"

"There were so many farm animals on the ship when we found it. Seems he had built a fire and tried to cook a cow he made, but he caught himself alight and… well you can guess,"

Camila just sunk back into her pillows and made sure she stared into her beautiful daughter's stunningly young eyes as she felt her heart and breathing slow down.

At least now she knew what had happened to her beautiful wooden man and at least she could now die in peace.

And she could finally see her wooden man again on the other side and this time they would have an eternity together.

Just like she always wanted.

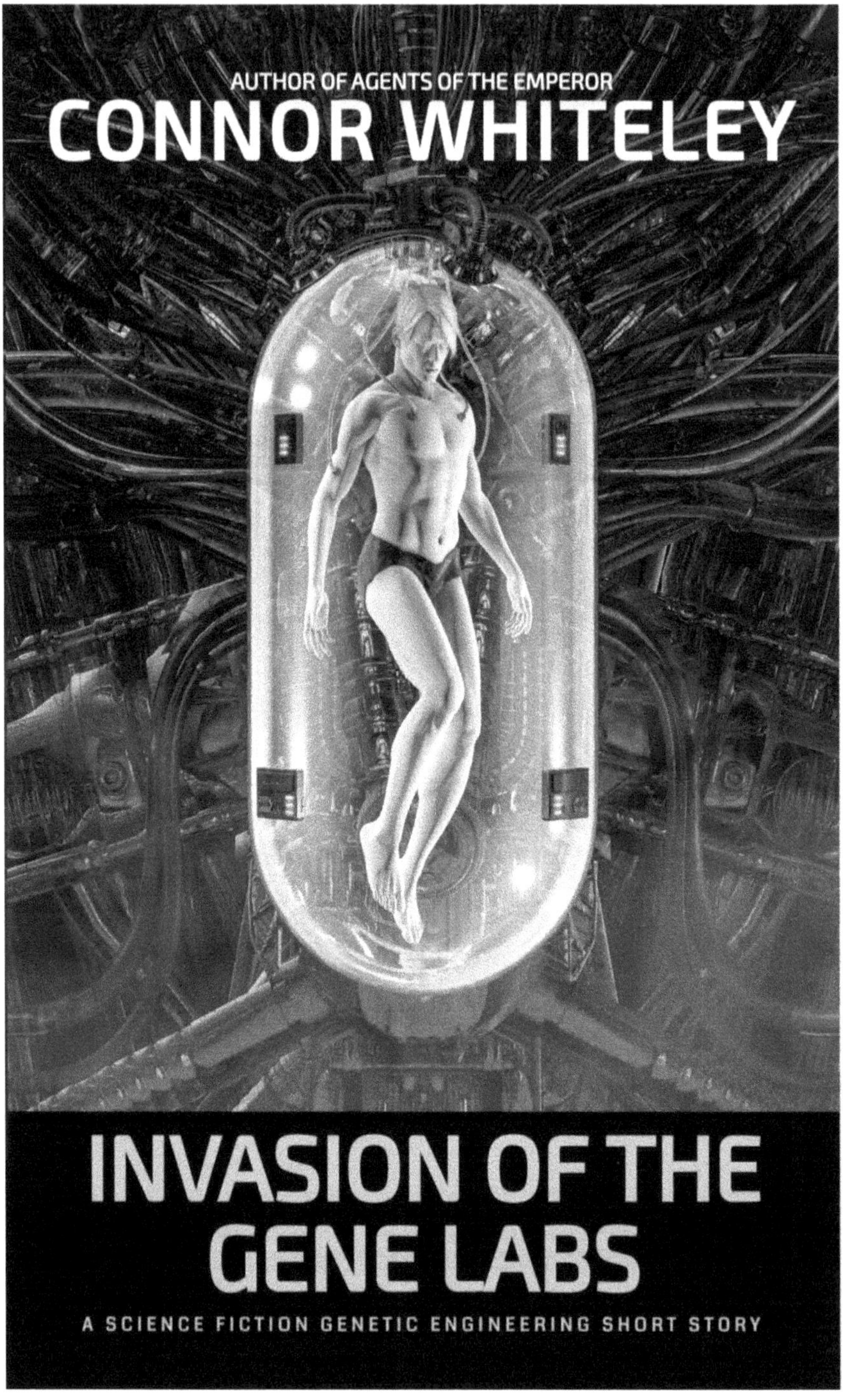
AUTHOR OF AGENTS OF THE EMPEROR
CONNOR WHITELEY
INVASION OF THE GENE LABS
A SCIENCE FICTION GENETIC ENGINEERING SHORT STORY

INVASION OF THE GENE LABS

Science Director Adam Fisher hated that today was the day his life would be changed in more ways than one. He would gain freedom from his ideas and he would learn the true horror of the galaxy.

He sat on his massive black, fabric director chair that his first-ever boyfriend had bought him over three years ago. It was a shame that the sweet young man was now dead, died on a forgettable planet winning in a battle that didn't matter now, but that was the way the Empire worked.

Adam had always liked how the black fabric chair had all the right support in all the right places, so much so that it felt like he was sitting on a cloud most of the time. Or like he was actually having a supportive hug for the first time in years, he really, really liked that supportive, loving feeling.

His blue holographic computer was activated in front of him and Adam had given up trying to look at all the streams upon streams of genetic information that was being shown to him. He understood it all but there was simply too much data for him to enjoy.

He turned off the computer and simply enjoyed the sheer silence of his massive oval office. He smiled to himself because no one else had ever liked his office, even his past boyfriends had said they hated the black walls, the white marble floor with purple veining running through it and even the endless holographic bookshelves scared them a little.

Adam wasn't exactly sure why but he liked it. This was his science lair, where he could create and tinker with grand genetic ideas and he could be transformed into the mad scientist he had always wanted ever since he was a kid.

The ceiling had to be his favourite part of the office. Adam had loved hand painting each little star on the black ceiling so it looked like he was outside. He supposed he could have easily brought himself a holo-projector to make an extremely realistic starry sky on the ceiling, but he liked doing things with his hands.

The sweet aromas of caramel, grapefruit and freshly roasted pecans filled the air, making the grand taste of pecan pie form on his tongue. He really liked it but the slight hint of smokey and charred flesh in the air reminded Adam of what was happening outside.

There was an invasion happening.

Adam shook his head as he reactivated his entire holographic computer and he double-checked what was happening. It seemed there were five small blade-like warships entering orbit of their moon base.

Adam had learnt a lot over the years from past boyfriends about the superhuman traitors and their baseline human slaves. He recognised these ships as belonging to the Divine Children, their evil black paint made that clear as day.

They weren't fighting just yet but it was only a matter of time.

Adam knew the loyalists on the immense blue, green and red planet below would send reinforcements in time but by the time they were here the entire moon could be annihilated.

He shook his head at the idea. This was all covered in basic training and the new security memo that came out last week.

The traitors might have recovered the technology to forge brand-new superhumans in recent weeks but they were still learning. And they wanted more data, more resources and more everything.

They wouldn't annihilate the lab until they had secured what they came for. It really was that simple.

Adam contacted the base's head of security. A moment later

Anna appeared in blue holographic form in front of him, she was already in her full heavy armour and carrying a sniper rifle in one hand and a missile launcher in another.

She had always been one tough woman.

"Anna," Adam said, "we have to buy as much time as possible so reinforcements can arrive. Concentrate on delaying tactics and protect the DNA samples and the labs at all cost,"

"Confirmed," Anna said clearly on the move. "What about Arcangel?"

Adam grinned. He had almost forgotten about his prized pet project that had been gifted to him by none other than Doctrine Catherine Taylor herself, the woman who created the superhuman Angels of Death and Hope. Also known as the Mother of Angels.

"Leave him to me," Adam said. "I can deal with him just buy me time,"

"if anyone can do this then you can," Anna said knowing she had to buy him time. "You're the man that can do this,"

Adam nodded and simply cut the line. He felt a little unsure of himself for a moment. It wasn't because of Arcangel because that should be theoretically simple even because he just had to complete the ritual to get him to come alive.

But it was getting called a man.

Adam had no idea why it irked him so much because he was a man but being called a man just didn't sit well with him. Sure he had always thought of himself as a man but… he just wasn't sure.

As an immense vibration ripped through the moon base, Adam just rolled his eyes because he really had to get moving. The traitors were here and he had labs to secure.

He clapped his hands and a long sword, a rifle and small pistol materialised in front of him. He picked them up and he simply went to war.

No traitors were surviving an invasion of his base today.

Not if he could help it.

***

Adam was so glad after spending ten minutes marching through the long, perfectly straight narrow corridors of the moon base, he had finally made it to the lab section.

The sheer hit of lemons, limes and grapefruits filled the air as Adam went inside the large white oval lab. Every single surface was perfectly sterile and everything was in its perfect place, or nothing was out of place.

There were ten long rows of small white lab tables with all sorts of genetic equipment on them. Adam could name all of them and he really wanted to see people's latest results but he had to secure his pet project.

Adam went through the lab making sure not to touch anything. The sheer silence of the lab was odd and it seemed alien compared to the normal busyness and sheer energy in the lab of excited scientist hoping to make their next great discovery to unlock the genetic power of the human genome.

Adam went to the very back of the lab where there was a perfectly smooth white wall without anything on it. There were posters, no projectors, no holograms. It was just a wall that was there to be looked at but ultimately ignored.

He tapped on the very centre of the wall briefly and then a slight humming filled the lab until a small glass pod floated down from the ceiling.

The lab jerked, vibrated and banged again as the traitors probably fired upon it.

He had to get Arcangel working now.

Adam went over to the pod and he was really impressed with how artful the sleeping superhuman was in their glass coffin. He looked so peaceful, sleepy and like he couldn't even hurt a fly.

Adam just admired the man's immense cheekbones and long black hair that might as well have been a lion's mane instead of human hair. The man had slight fangs and a real aura of power, death and deadliness.

Adam didn't really care too much about the killing power of the superhuman but he just felt something was different inside him. Whenever Adam looked at another man it wasn't always attraction he felt, he was actually seriously picky when it came to men but he always felt a sense of "otherness" like he was a male but he wasn't a man.

He certainly wasn't a woman but he wasn't a man either.

Adam shook away the idea and he simply went to the other end of the glass coffin and a yellow hologram appeared. He started typing in the different codes that he needed to enter to activate the sleeping superhuman.

Arcangel was meant to be the next kind of superhuman, faster, stronger, deadlier than anything humanity had ever seen before. But Adam just wanted to survive this, he didn't want to die at the hands of traitors so as much as he didn't know if this was ethical.

He just wanted to live.

"I wouldn't do that if I was you," a woman said coming over to him.

Adam looked at the woman and rolled his eyes. She was wearing a beautifully long black trench coat, black boots and her long black hair almost flowed around her.

And she was holding a gun to his chest.

"I am busy you know," Adam said. "And I do not appreciate the Divine Children attacking my base,"

"Well if you simply give me that Arcangel then we can go," the woman said leaning on the other end of the glass coffin.

"As if you have the authority to command such things and make such stupid promises," Adam said not liking this woman for a single moment.

"I am not a mere baseline human. I am a Talon of The Lord,"

Adam laughed. Everyone in the Empire knew exactly what the Talons of the Lord were, they were five superhumans that served as the advisors and executioners for the Lord of War. The evil bastard that controlled the traitors and wanted to enslave humanity.

Yet this woman was not a superhuman.

"Everyone knows only superhumans get on the Talons. You are not one so you are lying,"

The woman grinned at Adam as she took off her trench coat and revealed how the number 3 had been carved in her flesh over 333 times.

"I am the Third Talon of the Lord of War. I have burnt so many worlds, killed so many soldiers and I have gutted so many men like you,"

Adam laughed because it was hardly the time but he felt annoyed or disconnected when someone was calling him a man.

But maybe he could use that to his advantage.

He finished typing out the commands and the damn hologram mentioned how the Arcangel was activating but he wouldn't be ready for another five minutes.

Just typical. The one time Adam needed him awake he actually wasn't going to wake up for ages. The lazy bastard.

He had to buy time for himself.

"How do you think of me?" Adam asked walking away from the glass coffin in hope she would walk away too and not see him waking up.

"I see you as a pathetic Empire soldier that doesn't deserve to live," the woman said. "And my name is Ophelia Lockwood,"

"Could you have any more of a pompous name?" Adam asked.

The woman laughed. "That's funny and you are probably right. Yet because it is so pompous my victims always remember it as I kill them,"

The woman fired.

Adam jumped to one side.

"Relax sorry," Ophelia said. "I didn't realise my fingers were going to fire,"

Adam didn't have the heart to point out that she was the person who controlled her hands and arms and ability to shoot.

Adam didn't dare get up for now. All he wanted was to make sure he didn't die and that Arcangel was activated without a problem.

"Why did you ask about how I saw you?" Ophelia asked wanting Arcangel activated. "Most Empire idiots want to know my plan and how I will kill them,"

"We already know your plans. You want the DNA and lab samples so you can create more Superhumans,"

"True enough," Ophelia said.

Adam stood up and noticed she was heading back over to the glass coffin. He could only allow her to see that Arcangel was activating.

"Wait," Adam said. "I wanted to know if you see me as a man or woman or anything else,"

Ophelia smiled. "It doesn't matter if you're a man, woman, whatever. You all bleed the same so I can stab, shoot and gut you the same. I think there's an old human term *non-binary* or whatever. But my point remains I will kill you whatever you are,"

Adam didn't know exactly how to take that.

Ophelia went over to the glass coffin and laughed. "Ten seconds later that was a very nice distraction,"

Adam whipped out his pistol and Ophelia did the same. "You cannot harm him,"

Ophelia laughed. "Do not be so stupid,"

The glass coffin hummed as it cracked open and Arcangel stood up.

"You have no idea what Arcangel is do you? Arcangel was not a creation of Catherine Taylor, he was a creation of another woman with a lot more evil inside her. The Oddball of the galaxy she's called and when she created the Arcangel she gave him one purpose,"

Adam aimed his pistol at Archangel as he stood up and grinned. "What purpose?"

"To kill you all," Ophelia said.

Arcangel charged.

Adam fired. Bullets screamed through the air. Sheer terror gripped him.

Adam screamed. The bullets smashed into his armour.

Archangel flew at him.

Arcangel ripped up lab tables.

He smashed equipment.

He flew at Adam.

Adam backed into a corner.

The icy coldness of the wall shot into him.

Arcangel was a metre from him. He went to kill Adam.

A missile slammed into Arcangel.

Adam ran towards Anna in the doorway.

Arcangel roared.

Adam fired at him.

Anna fired missile after missile.

Adam dived out the labs.

He sealed the doors and he activated a cleansing procedure but he knew it was useless.

He certainly knew it was useless as a loud deafening bang echoed across the entire moon base. Adam activated his holographic display on his watch and he simply shook his head as he saw the traitors were in all retreat.

"They were always only here for Arcangel. They didn't care about the DNA samples and equipment," Adam said.

Anna shook her head. "Damn that's all. Is there was a kill code?"

Adam wasn't exactly sure what she was talking about but then he remembered the conversation he had had years ago with Doctor Catherine.

They had been sitting in his office with the enviro-systems pumping sweet scents of oranges, grapefruits and lemons into the office as they both drank lemonade together. They were both laughing and had had a great day together, and Adam's mind had been blown about three times by her extremely beautiful knowledge of human DNA.

But just before she had teleported away she had told him that Arcangel was being gifted to him because the superhuman was a big mess in itself. It wasn't friendly, it wasn't stable and it was simply doomed to die if it was ever reactivated.

"No kill code," Adam said to Anna, "but I don't think we need to stress too much about the Arcangel. I don't think he'll be much use to the traitors,"

Adam was about to go back to his office to report to Regional Command and take stock of what had happened to the base and what else had the traitors taken when Anna placed a loving hand on his wrist.

"And what about you? Who are you now?" Anna asked. "I listened to the conversation and everyone in the base knows your gender isn't a man. We're all geneticists by trade, we know gender is the social construct, biological sex is the concrete part."

Adam laughed as they didn't really know, or to be honest they didn't really know how to say it to Anna.

"I know now that I am not a man, I am certainly not a woman but I am me. I am Adam Fisher and I am just a person. I am a person that loves helping others, saving lives and simply being me," Adam said.

Anna smiled and hugged him. "And we all love you for being a great director and a person that could have doomed us all today but you didn't,"

Adam knew what Anna was talking about. It wasn't exactly uncommon for a Director of small bases to simply flee at the first spot of trouble but Adam wasn't like that. They loved saving others, and this was their home they weren't going to leave it and everyone else to suffer.

Adam simply smiled and them and Anna went back to their office. There was a lot to explore, a lot to report and a lot of damage to explain to Region Command but Adam didn't care. There might have been an invasion of the gene labs on the base but the traitors had wasted a lot of resources on a pet project that would die soon enough.

But the invasion had gifted them something a lot more precious. It had gifted Adam a real chance to finally know who they actually were and that was an amazing thing to realise after so long of not knowing and simply being unsure of themselves.

AUTHOR OF ACCLAIMED AGENTS OF THE EMPEROR SERIES
CONNOR WHITELEY
HUSBAND 100
A SCIENCE FICTION TIME TRAVEL SHORT STORY

HUSBAND 100

If there was anything that Historian Thomas Male flat out loved more than anything else in the entire world, it had to be the feeling, romance and ceremony of getting married, and he loved the holiday season even more.

A lot of his friends, family and past lovers had mentioned that they would have thought history was his greatest love after the holiday season, because in his original timeline he had never been married.

Well, that wasn't strictly true. He had been married only once for about a year before he moved to the London Historical Institute in the year 2500. Jason had been beautiful, very kind and Thomas had never ever met another mind like him. It was amazing how Jason just had such a unique way of seeing history, the present and how a single act in history could create a stunning ripple effect that would change the world forever.

And ultimately how humans never learnt from their mistakes. Thomas really enjoyed listening to Jason night after night until there was a mishap with the Time Water at the Glasgow Historical Institute so Jason became frozen in the water. He couldn't travel, couldn't move, couldn't anything.

Thomas was just glad he wasn't at the lab that day, so he moved to London, thankfully Scotland was independent by that point, and he wanted to continue his research.

With all the peacetime periods at his disposal, at first he wasn't entirely sure what period to focus his book on regarding same-sex marriages, families and holidays and their social, political and economic interaction. Okay, maybe he was planning a series of books but he wanted to get married and enjoy the past in alternative timelines. That was the best part about being a Travaler with the Time Water, each droplet represented a different timeline, a different past and a different way to manipulate events all without having an impact on his own timeline.

It was perfect.

A lot of his peers had mentioned why didn't he go back to the 2150s during the Indulgence Period when everyone was extremely rich and it was the Golden Age of modern society. He had considered it because the food was so fresh, so luxurious and so rich that nothing ever compared to those food, the soft, silky fashion and the sheer indulgence of the time period.

Others had mentioned he should go back to The Social War between 2359 and 2450 but he had heard enough about that time period from his grandparents and dad. To most people alive today, the Social War that was essentially a fascist war in all but name was history. To most of his family, it was memory.

He did not need to try and get married to a beautiful man during a war that wanted him dead.

He really didn't want to go through that. Especially as he would need to do this over and over to make sure he got enough research for his book series.

So he decided on the little-understood time period of the Third Carolean Age in the United Kingdom (back when it was sadly a United Kingdom) starting 2023 onwards until their King died in 2040.

His peers, friends and family couldn't understand why he would focus on marrying men in that time period, because there was a reason why no one studied it. Nothing really happened in that time period in the grand scheme of things. Sure, it led to the events of World War Three, the Western Curtain collapsing and the Global

Rise of The Fourth Power but all those wars happened in another fifty years.

2024 was unremarkable as far as history went.

And that was why Thomas wanted to study it. Peacetime was always the best time to study what a civilisation was actually like because there were no so stressors like war, famine and starvation like there were during the war times.

Yet ultimately it was the holiday decorations that Thomas flat out loved. He had heard of something strange called Tinsel that tinselled, sparkled and shone bright in its different reds, blues and greens when wrapped around a beautiful Christmas "tree".

So he travelled back in time over and over.

He always married the same sort of guy because he wanted a good research sample. He always married kind men that had good jobs that he could help with. The men never had to be stunning or movie-star quality because he cared and loved *them*, not their looks. He was marrying them because he loved *them*, he was never going to marry their looks or bodies.

Thomas only ever wanted to marry his boyfriend at the time for his personality, mind and everything he could teach Thomas about the past, Christmas traditions and more.

The first time he married was on 24th December 2024 to Jason Marks. A stunningly beautiful man with longish brown hair, a smile that could melt an entire room and a mind that was as sharp as a whip. Jason never went to university, unlike 2500 Jason, but he still managed to work as an impressive engineer at a major international delivery company.

The wedding was everything Thomas could have wished for and more. The entire church smelt of oranges, ground cloves and cinnamon. The great smell of pure Christmas that left the taste of mince pie on his tongue. All the pews were covered in red, copper and hot pink tinsel with a massive Christmas tree just behind the altar and even better there was a Santa Claus officiating the ceremony.

It was pure magic.

He was with Jason for forty years before the Rise of the Fourth Power happened and Jason was rounded up with so many others, so Thomas stayed to manage his three children and ten grandchildren before he returned to his timeline. Everyone was thankfully okay through the Rise but as far as his family was concerned Thomas was the last ever victim of the Fourth Power.

He didn't like them believing that but he had other timelines to explore.

When he rose up out of the Time Water, his 2080 jeans, dress shirt and hi-hop boots dripping wet, he couldn't help but smile because that was the first time he had ever tried to live an entire lifetime in the past.

He went back to his lonely box-like holo-office and he spent the next hour transcribing and dictating and downloading all his notes from his brain on Jason Marks, their children and everything he had learnt about the time period and he didn't even want to write up Jason's chapters yet.

He wanted to go back to the Time Water, and it was even better that only 5 minutes passed whenever he visited different Timelines. He could spend two minutes, two years or two hundred years in different timelines.

5 minutes would be the only amount of time to ever pass here, and he loved that about time travel.

He had wanted to go back into another timeline to find Jason Marks again and he could marry him over and over. Yet he supposed he needed to leave Jason alone in other timelines, Jason was perfect, stunning and clever as hell but there were other men like that too.

And he needed more research, more weddings and more fun times for his books.

So he went back into the timeline over and over because he loved the holidays, he loved getting married and he loved having a family for a few decades before he outlived everyone and he continued to a different timeline.

His twentieth husband might have been one of his favourite.

Stephen Craycraft was a seductive little twink about the same age as Thomas and he had never seen someone as stunning as Stephen before. He was a young university lecturer teaching computer science at Kent University.

Thomas was surprised that originally it was Stephen's fit, lean and small body that originally caught his attention at the university Christmas party that night. And the cute way how Stephen's brown hair was parted to the left was simply beautiful.

They had hit it off as soon as they saw each other, they had danced with each other constantly that night to more Christmas songs than Thomas knew existed and it was even better than Stephen wrapped copper tinsel around their waist whilst they danced so they *had* to be extra close to each other.

They married a year later on 26th December 2024 and he loved it. The ceremony wasn't done in a church thankfully and this time it was outside with only the refreshing warmth from burning chestnuts to keep them warm. The crunching snow was magical and the choir singing Christmas songs was everything Thomas had ever wanted.

It was another example of pure 2024 Christmas magic. This was why he loved traveling.

So again he spent another forty, sixty years with the stunning man he loved. Through all the troubles that history threw at them, all the drama of the Rise and even more so raising all their kids.

He really did love those kids and he had imparted his love of the holiday season into each of them like he did with all of his kids.

Then once Stephen died on an icy cold Christmas day in 2086, Thomas left without saying goodbye to anyone because losing Stephen really broke him.

Instead of spending an hour in his holo-office, downloading all his memories, notes and book ideas from his brain before heading back out into the Time Water. He actually spent a few weeks back in 2500. He wrote his first book, submitted it to the Institute so they could publish it for him and he had tried to meet some guys.

Yet the guys of 2500 were rich, a little arrogant and thankfully there was none of the "othering" that happened in the 2000s. Being gay was so normal that everyone was bisexual in 2500 and before traveling he flat out loved that because it's what allowed him to date a few guys back in school without any of the fear of rejection, bullying and worse that his husbands had experienced in 2024.

Yet he wanted the kindness, the awkwardness and how everything was harder in 2024 because they lacked the basic technology they took for granted now. Being a doctor wasn't that special in 2500 because their knowledge was so advanced that curing most illnesses was easy.

So after bedding a few guys, his book getting published and him wanting to get married again, Thomas went back into the Time Water over and over.

Of course it was completely fair at this point to say he was addicted to being married, the 2024 Christmas traditions and he loved being married at Christmas time. There was just something so magical about the coldness, the Christmas tree and the massive Christmas dinner that the English were obsessed with every year like clockwork.

The pigs in blankets had to be Thomas's favourite.

Yet after Husband 99 Thomas could have sworn he was done, so done in fact. Dylan Darling was the man who broke Thomas, because he was a stunning young man with long brown hair, a mixture of seductive masculine and feminine features that often made people wonder if he was a boy or girl and he was so clever. Thomas had always loved culture and understanding how social worlds worked, but Dylan was on a whole other level.

Neither of them had realised they were dating for the first six months because they were spending all their time together when they weren't working just talking, being together and discussing different cultures.

He was the only man he had ever considered telling that he was a Time Traveler.

So they married 25th December 2024 in the best ceremony ever and Thomas liked to consider himself an expert on wonderful weddings by now. There was no wedding cake this time, instead it was a massive Christmas cake filled with glace cherries, Italian mixed peel and freshly roasted pecans.

The entire wedding smelt of cinnamon, mulled wine and stollen, and there had been plenty of timelines where he had devoured the sweet, marzipan dish called Stollen like no tomorrow. It was so good.

Yet Dylan died of a heart attack on Christmas Day 2026. They barely managed to have a single child together and even that sweet, kind kid only made it to 21 years old, Thomas hated himself for that. He could have and should have taken Dylan to 2500 so he could be cured and everything could be worked out.

He couldn't be bothered to stay in Dylan's timeline for the Rise of the Fourth Power, he had seen the rise of fascism all over the world so many times now it was as mundane as watching paint dry so he returned to 2500 for the shock of his life.

When he returned, his 2026 jeans, dress shirt with the sleeves rolled up and his tennis shoes dripping wet, no one was in the lab. So he went over to the small kitchen area and directed a thought at the Food Synthesiser to make him a rich, turkey sandwich with wonderful sundried tomato pesto, basil and a fresh slice of melted cheese and he sat at the black marble table with gold veins running through it.

There was nothing better than the refreshing aroma of basil, tomatoes and juicy turkey, and it tasted even better.

After a few moments two very cute ladies stepped out of the Time Water holding hands, laughing and smiling about their latest adventure. Thomas offered them a turkey sandwich and he was scared they were going to shake his hand-off so he directed two more Thoughts at the Synthesiser and within minutes they were all sitting around the table together talking, laughing and catching up.

It turned out they were a couple who had been married three years in Real Time and they had spent over a thousand years in the past exploring the impact of the Social War in every single country on earth for those hundred years.

They still had a lot more countries to explore but they were so passionate, inspired and hopeful about their work that they didn't seem to care. He could relate. Thomas wasn't even sure how many hundreds or thousands of years he had spent in the past because it always took him a few months or years to find a man he wanted to marry in a given timeline.

He supposed he might have been traveling for close to a thousand years. That just stunned him, simply stunned him but he loved it.

Maybe not every single minute, and there were a good few husbands that he was never going to miss and there were plenty of amazing moments with each man.

The Time Water hissed a little and the most beautiful man Thomas had ever seen stepped out of the water in 2026-era jeans, a wedding suit and there was a Santa hat in his hand. Thomas didn't know what was more captivating first. The Santa hat? The guy's smile that could melt a room? The guy's striking piercing sapphire eyes?

Thomas could have sworn he had seen this man before recently. He didn't know where but as the cute man brushed his long black curls behind his ear he had a feeling it was in a different timeline.

He just had no idea which one.

"Lovely meeting you Thomas," one of the women said before her and her wife left for the showers.

Thomas smiled at the stunning man coming towards him and offered him a turkey sandwich which the man nodded.

"It just isn't the same as the 2024 rubbish, is it?" the man asked.

Thomas gasped and nodded and it took everything he had not to drop his mouth open. Now he knew exactly where he had met this man before. Dylan had a best friend, Peter, who was his Ex ex-boyfriend and he made odd comments about 2024 food not being perfect compared to when he had grown up.

Thomas had never questioned the comments until now, even though him and Dylan had laughed about it a few times.

"What is your name by the way?" the man asked. "You were Thomas Shields in the last one,"

Thomas laughed. "My name is Thomas Male, and what is your actual name?"

"Peter Higgins," the man said extending his hand and they shook and Thomas loved the chemistry, attraction and passion that flowed between them.

All Thomas wanted to do was kiss him, get to know him better and run his hand through all those lustrous curls.

"What were you researching?" Thomas asked. "And you do realise how much you hurt Dylan right by disappearing on us a few months before we got married,"

Peter looked to the ground. "I'm sorry about that. I study social factors leading to the election of the Fourth Power figures and I couldn't be in the same timeline as you anymore,"

Thomas leant closer. "Why? Did I hurt you or something?"

"No," Peter said. "Well, not really. I just… I wanted you to marry me instead because I've always liked you. It didn't matter if you were Thomas Green, Thomas Shark, Thomas with three other names. I have always liked you,"

Thomas was about to get up and walk away from Peter, he had clearly been creepy and followed him through the timeline but he realised that wasn't how the Time Water worked. The Time Water never allowed travellers to enter the same droplet of a timeline unless they were meant to be together.

It was a simple matter of physics.

"I never saw you in any other timeline," Thomas said. "It's a shame because… I really liked you too and Dylan always said what a great guy you were,"

"Yeah he was the only serious relationship I've ever had in the two thousand years I've been traveling in the past,"

Thomas finished off the last bite of his amazing turkey sandwich and offered his hand out to Peter.

"Well, give me an hour to download my notes and how about

we, you know, travel together for a little while? There's an amazing Italian restaurant in Canterbury in 2024 that does the best Christmas meal ever,"

Peter laughed. "Even now you still love the holidays. Me too. Sure, see you in another hour,"

And as Thomas watched Peter tuck another long curl behind his ear as he walked away, he couldn't deny he had a great feeling about this one. Peter was kind, amazing and Dylan had always said Peter was the second-best guy he had ever had the pleasure of meeting.

And if Peter was good enough for Dylan then Thomas didn't doubt Peter would make a brilliant husband 100, with a little training of course.

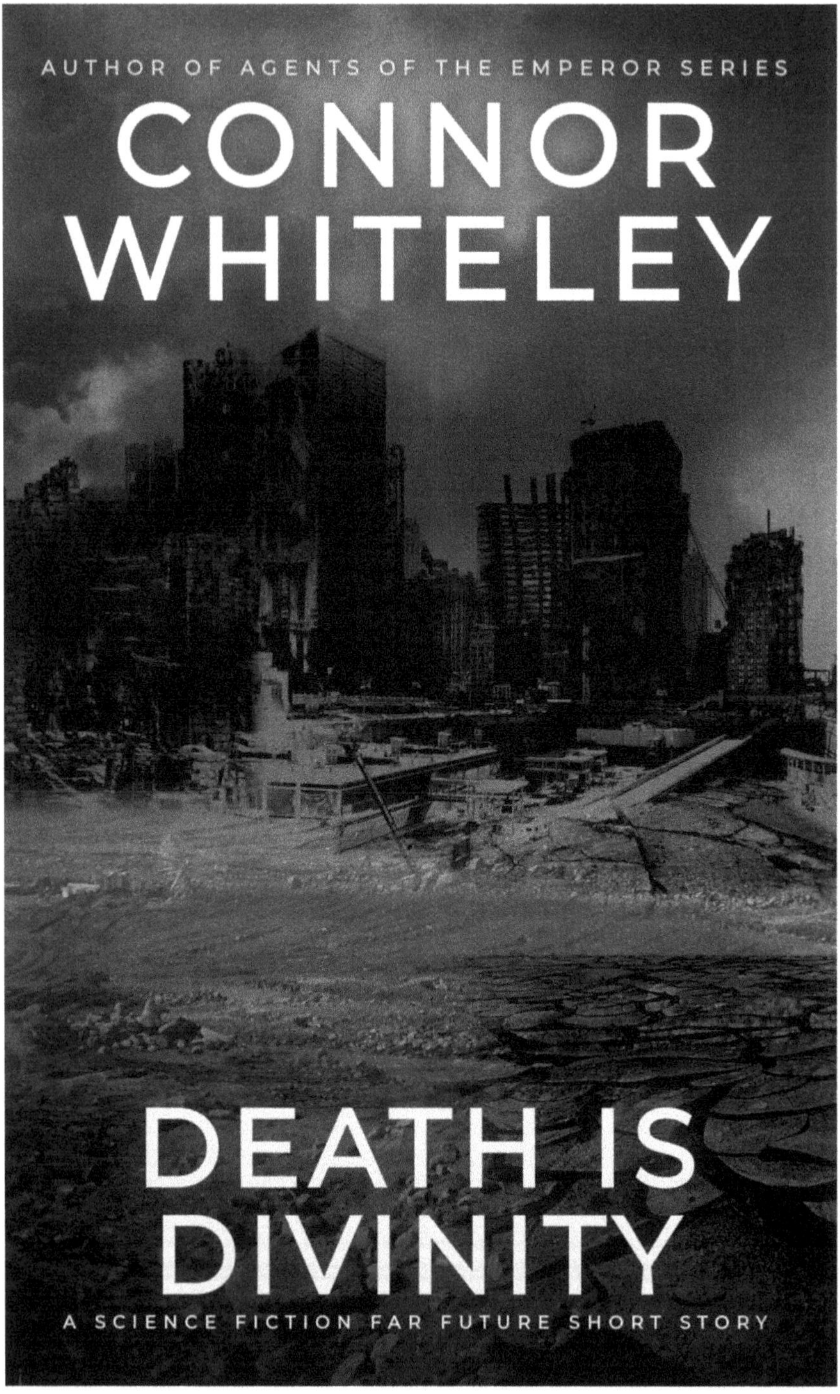
AUTHOR OF AGENTS OF THE EMPEROR SERIES
CONNOR WHITELEY
DEATH IS DIVINITY
A SCIENCE FICTION FAR FUTURE SHORT STORY

DEATH IS DIVINITY

This was the day I, Claire Clement, died and my true Goddess claimed my soul to stop the predations of the Death God from devouring and torturing me forever.

The awfully heavy noise of my own breathing filled my ears as did the humming, banging and vibrating of my rebreather mask as I stood in the middle of an ancient warehouse. The immense warehouse was easily big enough to fit two light cruisers inside and my breathing was probably barely loud enough to be more than a whisper in the sheer size of the place.

I hated how clouds of ash, toxic mould and the ash of corpses twirled, swirled and whirled around me as a cold wind blew through the entire warehouse. This wasn't a perfect position at all and I hated it, but I had to be here in service of my Goddess.

The immense grey metal walls of the warehouse were mostly destroyed now much like the rest of the planet. Large tears like claw marks had ripped into the walls like rotting flesh and pulled chunks out. According to my research this had once been a type of spaceport that delivered military supplies and food to the world.

All that was gone now and there wasn't meant to be anyone left alive here. That was of course a lie because I had already witnessed three very fresh corpses that hadn't even been touched by wildlife in the past hour.

Yet another reminder of the lies, deceit and chaos that bound the Imperium together. Yet I wasn't here for the Imperium of

Humanity and the foul Rex, I was here for my Goddess and I would do my duty to her no matter what.

Over a thousand years ago and even now, it was commonly believed that humans as a species cannot tap into the divine, the holy or the magical forces that pulse and flow and dance through every single living (and dead) thing in the galaxy.

I used to completely agree with that stupid, shallow opinion but growing up poor on a doomed farming world, left me wanting something, anything to cling onto. A lot of my friends turned to drugs, sex and criminal gangs to cope.

But I was extremely different, or so my friends and parents and the local Enforcers thought before they cut off my left hand.

I was playing around in a poor abandoned spaceport, a massively dusty, dirty circular creation that hadn't been touched in a hundred or so years, I found a book. It took me ages to understand it but it spoke of the Keres, a beautiful humanoid alien race, and their Gods and Goddesses I was fairly hooked immediately.

And I have tried to serve the Goddess of Life, Genetrix, ever since.

That service led me to the world of Ash 4.

I carefully started to go through the immense twirling, whirling and swirling masses of dirt and ash as I went deeper into the warehouse. In my service to Genetrix, I had learnt a lot over the years about the corruption of the Imperium and when I became an agent for the Enlighted Republic, a wonderful little breakaway region of humanity that believed in democracy, fairness and justice. I had learnt even more.

And there was something on this world that the Imperium wanted.

I stepped over a large chunk of metal wreckage that was unleashing a hell of a lot of heat towards me. I almost didn't want to step over it in case I burnt myself but I had to keep going.

The Republic had already sent three fleets of their extremely limited navy anyway, and none of them had returned. I had a good sense they had managed to make planetfall judging by the sheer destruction and how badly the planet was scarred.

All the ash and dirt stopped moving for a moment and I almost froze, surprised at the sheer stillness I felt, but I kept going careful to watch my step. There were tons upon tons of metal wreckage, old machinery and skeletons that covered the damn floor.

I focused on one particular machine for a moment as I passed it and it was some kind of massive drill, probably used for riveting or drilling the white metal sheets that the foul Imperial warships were famous for. I was glad it was destroyed.

The strange aroma of death, ash and smoke filled my senses as my own annoyingly heavy breathing continued in my ears. I had managed to use the data the Republic had gifted me and found that everyone was probably interested in a resource known as Gatix.

I had learnt about it in science class about two decades ago and it had only ever been found on three planets in the entire galaxy. It was meant to be this super strong, super conductive and super whatever you wanted. It was easy to programme if you knew what you were doing so if you had the material then you could do whatever. Including coat all your ships in the material to give them extreme levels of protection.

I didn't want the Imperium to have it. The Republic didn't want that, and I was fairly sure the alien Keres seriously didn't want that.

Something crashed behind me so I turned round and rolled my eyes as I saw bright white lights shine through the still clouds of ash and dirt. I had company.

I pulled out my gun from my waist out of my instinct, I normally forget about having it and I prepared to fight but thankfully my company decided to talk to each other and they hadn't noticed me yet.

"I keep telling you we should just annihilate this world," a woman said with a strange accent. "The Rex can have the Gatix like we promised but this world is useless,"

"You forget the true bargain that was struck," a man said but I couldn't understand his accent. "There is a spy here and this planet belongs to the Rex and humanity,"

My skin turned icy cold at the realisation that he was hunting me. I didn't want to be hunted, I didn't want to die, I only wanted to find the material and leave. It shouldn't have been that hard considering how tiny Gatix deposits were.

"Do you sense her?" the woman asked.

My own heavy breathing was replaced with the even more annoying sound of my pounding heartbeat. That stupid man had to be a Keres warrior, probably a Dark Keres dedicated to their Death God. Only someone with magic would be able to sense out people.

I immediately crouched behind a large metal piece of machinery in some silly effort to hide myself not that I really expected it to do much.

"I can sense her life force but it is strange for a human woman. It is almost like she believes in Genetrix," the man said.

I focused on the random movement of the light beams so I supposed my two hunters were certainly looking around for me now. They were going to find me so I just had to be ready.

Yet I couldn't understand what the Dark Keres meant about my soul. I believed wholeheartedly in the power of Genetrix. Sure I was only a human so I couldn't feel her, benefit from her magic or connect with her but I still believed in her. Because it was that belief that gave me so much strength, love and admiration for life in the galaxy.

And I needed some of that strength now because I was about to do something extremely ballsy.

I threw my voice across the warehouse. "Where is the Gatix?"

Both the light beams stopped moving and they both pointed in my direction so clearly I wasn't as good at throwing my voice as I thought.

"The Gatix is somewhere you will see very shortly," the man said behind me.

I went to spin around and shoot him but he whacked me over

the back of my head and my world went black.

***

When I eventually regained my senses, the first thing I sadly noticed was the sheer overwhelming aroma of burning petrol =You simply couldn't avoid the damn smell but I was surprised that I was freely standing on a massive red metal balcony overlooking tens upon tens of miles of pure annihilation.

For as far as I could see there was nothing except twisted wrecks of obliterated hab-blocks that looked like twisted metal corpses, entire warehouses and factories were reduced to ash and a lot more corpses than I even wanted to admit littered the tiny concrete streets like little dead ants.

The entire horizon was awful to look at and I couldn't help but wonder what Genetrix would say about this foul event. So much life had ended here, Genetrix would have grieved or cried or screamed out in bloody murder at what had happened here.

Even now small fires lit up the horizon with paper-thin lines of black smoke trying to veil the sky. There were rumours that Geneitor tried to use fire to devour the souls of his victims but I doubted it, I didn't want to believe it. I hated the very notion that he had been able to claim millions of souls from this single world and each soul only made him stronger.

And Genetrix, weaker.

I turned away from the awful horizon and just frowned at the tall Dark Keres standing there with his arms folded. I hated how humanoid they looked and I could only tell he was Keres and not a human because of his pointed ears, extremely thin waist and his pointed, almost angelic face.

It was amazing that the Keres were created by the Goddess of Life and yet some turned their back on her and joined the Death God that had created humanity.

Just behind the foul Keres was a large circular chamber with cracked black walls and a large holographic display of the planet, where a heavily armoured human woman was standing focusing on something I couldn't see. They didn't seem bothered by the smell but I wanted to cough or cover my nose, but I knew it would be useless.

And I didn't want to show weakness in front of these monsters.

"The Gatix, where is it?" I asked with a lot more force than I was used to.

The Dark Keres laughed. "I don't know why you care. You are going to die here, a faithless human who cannot possibly understand the War that is coming to this galaxy,"

"You are avoiding my question. The Gatix is a source of power that will help the Republic defeat you and the Imperium," I said focusing on the woman because I could see her smiling.

"The Imperium is a good employer but the Gatix will never reach them. The Dark Keres already have it," the woman said not daring to take her eyes off the holographic display.

The soul words hit me like bullets and my entire body felt so numb, so cold, so isolated. I had failed. My entire mission had been to find the Gatix and deny the enemy the chance to have it. Clearly I had been too late but I wasn't going to let the enemy win or claim a total victory.

I had to kill these two at least that would rob the enemy of two more foot soldiers in their awful war.

"I can sense your frustration," the Dark Keres said coming so close to me I could feel the icy coldness radiating off his twisted, spiky body armour. "How does it feel to know you believe in a Goddess that doesn't love you?"

I actually laughed at the dumb alien. That was the stupidest thing I had ever heard because my Goddess did love me, protect me and she was always with me. Sure I couldn't feel her, I couldn't channel her magic like the Keres or my soul couldn't be protected by her Divine Touch but she was always with me because I served her.

And no one else.

I reached to my waist and smiled as I realised my gun wasn't there but I had the power of Faith so I did not need a human gun to kill my enemy. I only needed a little time.

I had to find out what was going on with that holographic display.

"The display?" I asked carefully moving past the Dark Keres who was now making the air crackle with black magical energy. "What are you looking at? I didn't think there were any ships up in orbit,"

The human woman laughed. "Of course there are no ships in orbit. We would have called upon Geneitor to rip them away long before they reached their Drop Pod range. Yet there is a Dark Keres ship leaving the system,"

I smiled. I had to destroy that ship and make sure no one could easily access the Gatix and maybe in the far future the Republic could secretly send a recovery vessel to retrieve the Gatix from space.

I went over to the human woman and stood so close to her that I could smell her horrific body odour that made me want to vomit.

An icy cold blade pressed against my back.

"Do you not think I would know your intention human? There are extremely powerful weapons on this planet but that ship is leaving the system in one piece,"

I laughed hard. These dumb Keres and woman were telling me everything I needed to know because he made it sound like that Keres ship was still within range of the planet's defence systems. I had no idea if the defence systems were still intact but I had to try.

The human woman pointed a gun at my chest. I was trapped but I wasn't defeated because I was going to die for Genetrix even if I couldn't confirm if she was 100% real. She was real enough for me to believe in and that was okay.

I jumped back onto the Dark Keres's blade. Crippling pain shot through me. I screamed in agony.

The woman fired.

The bullet missed me.

The Dark Keres stumbled back. I elbowed him in the chest. The face. The ribs.

He fell to the ground.

I spun around.

Jumping on his head.

His head cracked like an egg. I felt warm blood rush down my back. I saw the blade in the Keres' hand.

A bullet screamed through the air.

I rolled forward.

Grabbing the blade from the Keres.

I spun around.

I threw the blade at the woman's chest.

The blade rammed itself into her chest and the gun fell from her hand. She staggered back and forth as she collapsed to the ground.

Even worse she was stupid enough to actually rip the blade out so the blood could flow quickly out of her body. So I went over to her dying body and snapped her neck so she could have a quicker death.

"May the Mother of Life protect your souls from the predations of the Death God," I said knowing these awful enemies didn't deserve such a kindness.

I went to take a step forward but I almost collapsed as I felt more and more warm blood roll down my back and legs and even a small trail was forming on the metal floor.

I forced myself over to the holographic display and zoomed in on the Dark Keres ship that was almost out of range. I tapped on the hologram and it brought up all sorts of sensory outputs and information.

There was a piece of holographic text that highlighted that it was a friendly ship so I pressed it and changed the setting to Enemy. The entire hologram buzzed, crackled and popped and then several systems popped up including missiles, bombs and other defensive measures.

I clicked launch and the entire planet vibrated and shook violently as missile silos, laser batteries and so many other defence systems across the entire planet activated. I suspect most of the missiles were annihilated as they hit several chunks of rumble that covered the silos but I saw at least twenty missiles light up the sky.

The hologram flashed a few times as the missiles accelerated once they reached the void and within thirty seconds the Dark Keres ship was obliterated.

I was going to smile but I sunk to my knees as I didn't have the blood nor the strength to stand. I wanted to call the Republic and tell them what had happened, how they could recover the Gatix but I couldn't. There simply wasn't enough time.

But it was okay because I was going to die in the service of Genetrix and everything would be just fine. This was Her will after all and she would guide and twist fate as she deemed right, so if she deemed the Republic the best people to have the material then she would Will it.

I sunk to the icy cold metal floor as the last of my life was drained away from me I just grinned as I saw a warm golden light and I knew, just knew that my Goddess was real and she was finally going to claim my soul as a thank you for my service, my loyalty and my determination to protect all innocent life.

AUTHOR OF AGENTS OF THE EMPEROR
CONNOR WHITELEY
TERRA IS NOT EARTH
A SCIENCE FICTION SPACE OPERA SHORT STORY

TERRA IS NOT EARTH

As an Empire Intelligence Officer, I've heard a lot of weird things in my service to the Emperor and the Great Human Empire. I've heard of aliens with wings that walk everywhere, I've heard of upside-down worlds where it rains upwards, and I have heard of planets run by humanoid babies.

I've heard a lot of weird stuff in my time, but this just might be the weirdest in my career, let alone the history of the Empire Intelligence Bureau.

Or even the Inquisition.

As I, Hailey Knight, went down a long, narrow black corridor made up of thousands of constantly shifting metal plates the size of fingernails, I couldn't help but hiss as my stomach churned at the news my aide had delivered. We had a prisoner who reported they could confirm that Terra was real.

And that Terra was not a reference for Earth.

The corridor was choking and overwhelming with its horrible aroma of blood, burnt flesh and burnt hair that lingered on my long black trench coat like its life depended on it. It was why I never came down to these lonely levels, that I left to interrogators and lessers.

Now I was probably going to have to burn my trench coat. A shame considering my Mum gave it to me before I killed her for heresy.

I continued down the corridor and the long thin white line of lights above me flickered, popped and banged. The entire corridor was sadly groaning as if I was so heavy I was actually straining the metal structure.

Please believe me when I say this isn't true, it's all part of the psychological warfare we wage against our prisoners. We play them scary sounds, we make the floor levels vibrate and we even make the prisoner believe there are starving cyber-hounds outside just waiting to break in and eat them.

We naturally do all of this after we give them a nice little injection to increase the sensitivity of the nerve endings, make the fear responses a little more extreme and something to make their heart pound in their chest. Of course some people die of a heart attack within their first day here or first hour, but they deserve it.

These are all criminals after all.

I turned a sharp right and started to go down an even longer and narrow black corridor with tens of thousands of constantly moving metallic plates. It was enough to make you sick and make your head spin but I was here with a purpose.

The aroma of dried metal clung to the air making the awful taste of iron form on my tongue. I normally only had that taste after fights or on the rare occasion my investigations took me to a war zone. I was hardly impressed I had the taste of iron in my mouth on Earth itself.

The Throneworld of the Empire and the birthcradle of humanity.

And now I had a prisoner saying that Terra was real. A fact that could rock the foundations of the entire Empire if that was true.

It's a well-known fact that the Empire is at war with the superhuman traitors. 6 entire legions of superhuman warriors turned against the glorious light of the Emperor, and 3 remained loyal. The traitors followed the Lord of War wanting to enslave humanity and rule the Empire under his evil, iron grip.

I fight for the freedom of humanity.

The entire prison groaned even more and I could have sworn I heard the patting of metal feet behind me as if I was prey being stalked.

I placed a hand on the cold metal grip of my gun. I was not being prey in my own prison.

The problem with the superhuman traitors is that we aren't really sure where their Throneworld is. We know the traitors have established their own Imperium, we know they rule over tens upon tens of worlds and we know the region of space.

We just have no idea where their Throneworld is.

This prisoner claims to know that critical information.

About 60,000 years ago, a few years after the Civil War began and the Lord of War revealed his true self, we started hearing words and a single planet being referenced. We thought it was another name for Earth and the Emperor but over the next few thousand years we realised that was wrong.

Terra.

It was the same reference being said over and over again like it was the most holy and most important planet in existence.

Again we thought they were talking about us and Earth, but that was impossible. A few of us, like myself, believe that this isn't Earth and the Inquisition in all their secrecy and shadows probably agreed with us. But the larger Empire does not.

It's why I was demoted so many times.

But when an old friend of mine from the Empire Navy mentioned he picked up a prisoner referencing Terra, and said the prisoner was happy to speak to Empire Authorities. Well, I got interested and that brings me here.

I stopped in front of a massive churning, vibrating, popping mess of wall with all the black metal plates swirling. The entire metal structure groaned like the prison was about to collapse and I didn't know if I was about to be deafened.

I raised my hand but then it all stopped.

"Intelligence Officer Hailey Knight accessing prisoner," I said to the wall.

The metal plates all zoomed to the sides, I stepped inside and then the metal plates sealed me in with a deafening roar and laughter and giggle.

"Who are you?" a man asked.

I ignored the man for a moment and focused on the type of cell my aide had authorised for the prisoner. It was a little nicer than I normally order for my prisoners. This cell was easily 2 metres by 2 metres with a cold metal shelf with a bed with rusty chains holding it to the wall.

There were no leaks, no drafts and no pillows. It was literally just an empty boxroom with only the metal shelf attached by chains to the wall. I would have preferred the man to have a leaky one, so maybe he could have battery acid, urine or even toxic chemicals dripping on him as he fell to sleep.

That always got the guilty talking and begging me for mercy.

And sometimes I gave it to them with a bullet or I sent them half away across the galaxy to earn the Emperor's forgiveness by dying on some forgettable world.

"I said who are you?" the man asked again.

I looked at him this time but I didn't dare say anything. I wanted to make him uncomfortable, and he was hardly bad-looking. His grey prison jumpsuit was a little slashed up and stained with small blood droplets of blood, so clearly his jumpsuit hadn't been washed before it was given to him.

His cruelly cut brown hair was sort of styled into a cute crewcut and it framed his handsome face perfectly. I could tell by his eyes that he was scared, concerned and he had no idea if he could trust me.

I liked that in a man.

"I am Intelligence Officer Hailey Knight of the Emperor's Intelligence Bureau. You have exactly one shot to convince me of your information and then I, and I alone, will decide your fate," I said.

"EBI," the man said like he knew the name. "I always thought I would be questioned by the Inquisition,"

I forced myself not to take a step back and I noticed his strong, choking body odour and intoxicating manly musk for the first time. If what he said hadn't scared me so much, I might have allowed myself to be a little aroused.

No normal person in the Empire, or traitors for that matter, actually knew or spoke about the Inquisition. They were a cold, calculating top-secret organisation that were laws upon themselves and had the power to burn entire worlds and trillions of people on a whim.

It was beyond strange this man wanted to talk to one of them.

Whoever this man was he was not a mere man like my old friend had made him out to be.

"Tell me your information," I said with as much authority as I could.

"No, I will watch you panic, watch you get scared and watch you beg me for my information. I know you know that I am telling the truth,"

"You have not told me any truths so far," I said glad I still had a hand on the cold grip of my gun.

"I can smell your fear little one," the man said licking his lips. "You want to examine me, you are so desperate for my information that you didn't bother checking the basics,"

I took a few steps away from him and as I realised there was something very wrong with his body odour and manly musk. I had had more than enough military boyfriends that loved to have sex after training. I knew exactly what manly musk smelt like and this musk was wrong.

It was artificial, chemical and it was almost like it was trying to hit every single pleasure cell in my brain. Like someone knew exactly what I loved and got me aroused and someone was targeting that part of me.

I whipped out my gun and trained it on his forehead.

I had to have missed something, anything. My old friend had contacted me, explained the situation and I had dispatched my aide to run the preliminaries. He had confirmed the prisoner and case was real and then…

I had broken protocol slightly by not dealing with a prisoner directly once the ship reached the docks. My old friend hadn't used standard EBI procedures when transferring the prisoner and my aide had never really confirmed why this was classed as a low-level case.

This should have been an Alpha-Case with top-level security, interrogation and torture techniques. This prisoner should have received a lot more interest than it did, and I hadn't figured it out until now because I was distracted writing up a report.

And I was too eager for a future promotion.

"Now you get it," the man said.

The man started manically laughing. He laughed over and over and his face melted away, the entire metal structure groaned in protest and the man grew.

I fired.

By the Emperor did I fire.

My explosive rounds screamed through the air. Smashing into the man's forehead again and again.

It should have obliterated his body twenty times over.

Then I realised exactly what he was turning into. I watched as the human male that was no taller than a standard baseline human grew into a superhuman, 3 metres tall, wearing the jet black armour of the Raven Crow.

Superhuman infiltration specialists.

"And now you have led me straight into the heart of the EBI headquarters little human," the superhuman said.

My ears bled as his booming voice echoed off the smooth black walls. The aroma of burnt ozone and electrical discharge filled the cell and he charged at me.

But I was an EBI officer.

I rolled to one side.

He slammed into the wall behind me.

He punched. Kicked. Swung at me.

I dodged.

He punched at me.

Again.

Again.

He was fast.

Too fast.

I rolled away.

Again.

Again.

Trying to be as random as possible.

He went to kick me. I jumped in the air but he changed his attack a moment before I could change mine.

He grabbed me.

Slamming me against the wall.

The deafening groan of thousands of tonnes of metal echoed all around me and the superhuman just laughed.

"See little human, you think you are so clever trying to stop us. You think you can win against the Lord of War but you cannot. We are everything, nowhere is safe from the touch of the Raven Crow nor the Hydra Legion. The Raven infiltrates and the Hydra spies on all,"

I seriously hated superhumans.

I tried to claw his grip off my neck but it was useless. My hands looked tiny and pathetic against his massive armoured hands. I didn't doubt he could snap my neck with the smallest of movements.

I just wanted to live, protect humanity and fight for freedom.

"What do you want?" I asked.

"Your brain will tell me everything I need to know," the superhuman said placing his other hand on the top of my skull.

My eyes widened as I realised how superhumans could eat the brains of their victims to learn all their secrets, all their memories and all their fears.

I screamed out in agony as the superhuman started to crack my skull to eat my brain.

I kicked. Punched. Struggled.

Then the superhuman stopped and he looked behind us and I could have sworn I heard the sound of tens of metal feet tapping on the cell door.

I raised my hand.

"EBI Officer Hailey Knight requesting access to the prisoner,"

The door melted down and I gasped as I saw twenty massive wolves with tiny little silver blades for hair and fur. And immense dagger-like teeth for fangs and their entire bodies were made from machines.

Their cold robotic eyes looked at me then the superhuman then me again.

"Kill this traitorous abomination," I said.

The wolves' eyes turned blood red and they charged.

I swung my gun. Smashing the superhuman on the head.

He dropped me.

I just got the hell out the way as the roars, screams and chomping of robotic jaws on superhuman flesh echoed around me.

***

A few hours later after EBI security had investigated the entire prison and made it secure, found the dead body of my old friend and freed my aide from the mind-control device the traitorous bastard had installed in him. I just stood in the middle of the cold, black prison cell focusing on the wrecked remains of the Raven Crow operative's armour.

Dark red blood painted the walls and floor of the cell and the rusty chains had finally broken so the "bed" was just a sheet of rusty metal on the floor now. It would never be replaced because it would be wrong to give heretics any kind of respect.

The aromas of blood, burnt flesh and hair still choked out the small cell as I still had the cell door open, but I preferred the smell to the fake manly musk. Even though I could do without the taste of rusty iron on my tongue.

I picked through the wrecked chunks of armour with some gloves in case they were coated in poison or something, and that was when I came across a small glowing blue bottom inside the helmet.

Against my better judgement I pressed it and I was stunned. A large red hologram appeared of a large version of Earth with thousands of pieces of data, data streams and facts surrounding it.

I didn't have time to understand all of it but I got the jist, and it would change the fate of the EBI, Inquisition and Empire forever.

This was Terra.

There wasn't a location or a name of a solar system, but the information explained that Terra was the capital world of the traitor forces, the seat of the Lord of War's power and where the Aresian Senate was located.

I felt like my mind wanted to explode because this contradicted tens of thousands of years of intelligence, social and political theory about how the traitor forces operated. They actually had a centralised place of power that if destroyed could wipe them out forever.

And ensure humanity and the Empire remained free.

The helmet exploded and the hologram died.

But I didn't care because I had everything I needed and I could now tell the Empire the truth about the traitors. And ultimately, I would be the person that started the next great stage of the Civil War, for tens of thousands of years, we had been fighting on the backfoot against the traitors just trying to survive.

Now we could take the fight to the traitors, win this war forever and ensure our freedom.

All because we had finally confirmed and learnt and proven that Terra is not Earth.

GET YOUR FREE SHORT STORY NOW! And get signed up to Connor Whiteley's newsletter to hear about new gripping books, offers and exciting projects. (You'll never be sent spam)

https://www.subscribepage.io/garrosignup

About the author:

Connor Whiteley is the author of over 60 books in the sci-fi fantasy, nonfiction psychology and books for writer's genre and he is a Human Branding Speaker and Consultant.

He is a passionate warhammer 40,000 reader, psychology student and author.

Who narrates his own audiobooks and he hosts The Psychology World Podcast.

All whilst studying Psychology at the University of Kent, England.

Also, he was a former Explorer Scout where he gave a speech to the Maltese President in August 2018 and he attended Prince Charles' 70th Birthday Party at Buckingham Palace in May 2018.

Plus, he is a self-confessed coffee lover!

Other books by Connor Whiteley:

Bettie English Private Eye Series

A Very Private Woman
The Russian Case
A Very Urgent Matter
A Case Most Personal
Trains, Scots and Private Eyes
The Federation Protects
Cops, Robbers and Private Eyes
Just Ask Bettie English
An Inheritance To Die For
The Death of Graham Adams
Bearing Witness
The Twelve
The Wrong Body
The Assassination Of Bettie English
Wining And Dying
Eight Hours
Uniformed Cabal
A Case Most Christmas

Gay Romance Novellas

Breaking, Nursing, Repairing A Broken Heart
Jacob And Daniel
Fallen For A Lie
Spying And Weddings
Clean Break
Awakening Love
Meeting A Country Man
Loving Prime Minister
Snowed In Love
Never Been Kissed

Love Betrays You
Love And Hurt

Lord of War Origin Trilogy:
Not Scared Of The Dark
Madness
Burn Them All

Way Of The Odyssey
Odyssey of Rebirth
Convergence of Odysseys
Odyssey Of Hope
Odyssey of Enlightment

Lady Tano Fantasy Adventure Stories
Betrayal
Murder
Annihilation

Agents of The Emperor
Deceitful Terra
Blood And Wrath
Infiltration
Fuel To The Fire
Return of The Ancient Ones
Vigilance
Angels of Fire
Kingmaker
The Eight
The Lost Generation
Hunt
Emperor's Council

Speaker of Treachery
Birth Of The Empire
Terraforma
Spaceguard

<u>The Rising Augusta Fantasy Adventure Series</u>
Rise To Power
Rising Walls
Rising Force
Rising Realm

<u>The Fireheart Fantasy Series</u>
Heart of Fire
Heart of Lies
Heart of Prophecy
Heart of Bones
Heart of Fate

<u>City of Assassins (Urban Fantasy)</u>
City of Death
City of Martyrs
City of Pleasure
City of Power

<u>Lord Of War Trilogy (Agents of The Emperor)</u>
Not Scared Of The Dark
Madness
Burn It All Down

Miscellaneous:
Dead Names
RETURN
FREEDOM
SALVATION
Reflection of Mount Flame
The Masked One
The Great Deer
English Independence

OTHER SHORT STORIES BY CONNOR WHITELEY

Mystery Short Story Collections
Criminally Good Stories Volume 1: 20 Detective Mystery Short Stories
Criminally Good Stories Volume 2: 20 Private Investigator Short Stories
Criminally Good Stories Volume 3: 20 Crime Fiction Short Stories
Criminally Good Stories Volume 4: 20 Science Fiction and Fantasy Mystery Short Stories
Criminally Good Stories Volume 5: 20 Romantic Suspense Short Stories

Connor Whiteley Starter Collections:
Agents of The Emperor Starter Collection
Bettie English Starter Collection
Matilda Plum Starter Collection
Gay Romance Starter Collection
Way Of The Odyssey Starter Collection
Kendra Detective Fiction Starter Collection

Science Fiction Short Story Collections
Rivetingly Great Stories Volume 1
Rivetingly Great Stories Volume 2
Rivetingly Great Stories Volume 3
Rivetingly Great Stories Volume 4
Rivetingly Great Stories Volume 5

Mystery Short Stories:
Protecting The Woman She Hated
Finding A Royal Friend
Our Woman In Paris
Corrupt Driving
A Prime Assassination
Jubilee Thief
Jubilee, Terror, Celebrations
Negative Jubilation
Ghostly Jubilation
Killing For Womenkind
A Snowy Death
Miracle Of Death
A Spy In Rome
The 12:30 To St Pancreas
A Country In Trouble
A Smokey Way To Go
A Spicy Way To GO
A Marketing Way To Go
A Missing Way To Go
A Showering Way To Go
Poison In The Candy Cane
Kendra Detective Mystery Collection Volume 1
Kendra Detective Mystery Collection Volume 2
Mystery Short Story Collection Volume 1

Mystery Short Story Collection Volume 2
Criminal Performance
Candy Detectives
Key To Birth In The Past

<u>Science Fiction Short Stories:</u>
Their Brave New World
Gummy Bear Detective
The Candy Detective
What Candies Fear
The Blurred Image
Shattered Legions
The First Rememberer
Life of A Rememberer
System of Wonder
Lifesaver
Remarkable Way She Died
The Interrogation of Annabella Stormic

<u>Fantasy Short Stories:</u>
City of Snow
City of Light
City of Vengeance
Dragons, Goats and Kingdom
Smog The Pathetic Dragon
Don't Go In The Shed
The Tomato Saver
The Remarkable Way She Died
Dragon Coins
Dragon Tea
Dragon Rider

<u>All books in 'An Introductory Series':</u>

THE FORENSIC PSYCHOLOGY OF THEFT, BURGLARY AND OTHER CRIMES AGAINST PROPERTY
CRIMINAL PROFILING: A FORENSIC PSYCHOLOGY GUIDE TO FBI PROFILING AND GEOGRAPHICAL AND STATISTICAL PROFILING.
CLINICAL PSYCHOLOGY
FORMULATION IN PSYCHOTHERAPY
PERSONALITY PSYCHOLOGY AND INDIVIDUAL DIFFERENCES
CLINICAL PSYCHOLOGY REFLECTIONS VOLUME 1
CLINICAL PSYCHOLOGY REFLECTIONS VOLUME 2
Clinical Psychology Reflections Volume 3
CULT PSYCHOLOGY
Police Psychology

A Psychology Student's Guide To University
How Does University Work?
A Student's Guide To University And Learning
University Mental Health and Mindset